Part1:
Powerless

Niall McCreanor

To John,

The only superhero I have ever known.

Jacinta and Oisín,

My reason for being.

ACKNOWLEDGMENTS

I would like to thank Jacinta Moonan, Gerard Sands, Seamus McKenna, Noelle McCreanor, Niall Busby, Dr. Marty Reilly, David Carolan, Paddy Hall and Andrew Hanratty for helping to guide me through the creative process.

CHAPTER ONE

White knuckled, Lee gripped the armrests of his chair – the centrepiece of his virtually empty apartment. He turned the volume of the ballgame on the TV up to full to help drown out the abrasive noises coming through the ceiling, but they became increasingly difficult to ignore. Lee could feel his heart rate speeding. This wasn't a new situation to be in, but neither was it one that he would ever get used to. He and his brother, Tom, had been brought up alone by their dad, so his experience of arguing parents was based purely on the friends he had visited, which admittedly was few and far between. But even so, he knew that the heart-wrenching cries of the young woman upstairs, accompanied by the ominous baseline of her husband's terrorizing taunts was not normal in any household.

Lee tried to block it out and focus on his plans for the day. It was his day off and the pressure was on to do something with it, to be productive before the onslaught of his job at the local newspaper weighed him down. Tomorrow he would have a mountain of articles to fact check and proof read before they would inevitably be scrapped for a nice family-friendly story. But he already felt weighed down. A day to celebrate his life. Yeah, maybe for some, but for him it had always felt like celebrating the death of his mother. Because let's face it, if he hadn't been born she would still be alive. Lee let his head fall back onto the cushion behind him and redirected his brain down a different route. He knew what he got like when he became lost in these thoughts. His problems with control were hard to mask, especially when idiots like the guy upstairs were concerned. Just as his heartbeat calmed the sudden sound of fist striking plaster jerked his head up. He listened carefully as the silence coming from upstairs spoke volumes to him.

Lee knew how this normally went. She had done something, probably pathetically inconsequential and her husband had exploded, no doubt taking his own self esteem issues out on her. Usually it was just shouting and crying and the odd door slamming, but he knew it was a more serious situation. There was always more going on than he might guess from the shouting he heard. He had seen the subtle pull of a sleeve over a bruised wrist as they passed in the corridor and the way her head hung a little lower when she walked behind her husband. She would probably be quite attractive if she washed her hair and pulled it back from her face, but Lee never looked for too long, for fear of what he might do to her. He didn't even know her name, but he'd heard her mutter her husband's name, Jimmy, in a quiet childlike voice often enough. There was no knowing what he might be capable of, and all too often, as Lee had learned on the playground, people only showed their powers when you least expected it. She must have a defensive power, he had told himself, thinking that surely a woman would protect herself when faced with an abusive man, if she could.

The walls must be paper thin, he thought, as the sounds of her whimpering drifted down to him. He could hear her husband saying something, but his voice was so deep he couldn't quite tell exactly what. But this time she answered him back and the response was instant. Perhaps a vase thrown or a shattered plate, but the sound of it clattering against the wall made Lee rise from his seat, his heart beating in his ears. With knees slightly bent and fists clenched, he was ready to move. Today there was a shadow resting over him and if this idiot next door wanted to push him, then he deserved to feel the full force of his fury.

A guttural scream propelled him to the door, but he ambled up the stairs and nervously knocked on the door, knowing there would be a confrontation but not knowing what really lay on the other side.

Lee continued to knock, muttering out loud, " H… Hello!" There was no response "Is everything ok in there?" Again his question was only met by silence. Filling up with an equal measure of confidence and rage Lee now banged on the door and assertively shouted, "Open up!"

Ignored again, Lee reached his hand down to try the handle on the door. Locked. The loud crash of what could only be a small woman onto a piece of furniture kicked Lee into action. Rage overwhelmed him and any hesitance dropped away as his instincts took over and he became a passenger to his own training. Planting his foot on the ground Lee raised his other leg, leaned back and kicked the door clean off its hinges. His keen eyes saw everything as he took in the scene unfolding before him. The place was a complete mess, whisky and beer bottles littered the living area. He entered the apartment and followed the abusive screams to the kitchen. Pushing open the door, his eyes moved straight to the girl cowering on her knees, a clump of her hair caught in Jimmy's fist as he bent over her screaming into her face.

The intensity of the fight blinded Jimmy to the intruder in their home, allowing Lee to make his move before the neanderthal had a chance to put up his defences. Lee moved behind him, placing one knee in the centre of his back and sweeping his elbow under the guy's arm and neck, holding him there as he released the hair his hand was clutching onto. Quickly the woman pushed herself along the floor, with her back to the wall, staring at this quiet yet familiar stranger in her home. Lee watched her move away before he made his next move, but Jimmy was one step ahead of him. Out of nowhere a mug came flying at his head. He ducked just in time but felt it splintering into pieces as it hit his shoulder.

He looked around the room trying to gauge if there was a fourth person in there with them, but instead the refracted light of the tail of an electric whip caught his eye as it lassoed a vase, throwing it towards Lee.

Pushing Jimmy to the floor, Lee landed a kick powered by the full weight of his body into the centre of his chest, giving himself a moment to work out what was going on.

The refracted electric strip of light appeared again, this time tossing a small table in his direction, but Lee had the chance to see the source of the light – Jimmy – or more specifically, Jimmy's wrist. So this was his power. He kept his distance, still unsure of the extent of this ability. He'd never seen anything like it before, but then again, everyone's power was always slightly different.

Jimmy paused for a moment as the pain of Lee's kick still tremored through his torso, but within a flash was hauling his body upright, taking in Lee with one long sweeping gaze.

"What the HELL are you doing here?!" he yelled, his voice like gravel. Turning to his wife with a disgusted sneer, his voice sank a notch lower, "Have you been talking to this one as well, you're pathetic!"

She looked between the two men and pushed her body further into the wall, seeking solace in its hard protection against her back. The light flickered around her, ever so slightly. Lee kept his body turned towards Jimmy, aggression screaming from every muscle, but moved his head ever so slightly, watching the air around the woman flicker. A forcefield, it's got to be. Well, at least he wouldn't have to worry about protecting her, as he beat the life out of her husband. She must really love this idiot if she didn't even use her own power to protect herself from him. Maybe that's what love did to you though. He focused his eyes on Jimmy, shaking off the melancholy thoughts and tuning into the obscenities he was shouting at his wife. He could almost see the pain hit her as each word landed, the forcefield offering no protection from them.

Jimmy whipped his arm towards Lee and a ribbon of light passed across the room, wrapping around Lee's waist, pinning his arms to his side. The harder he fought the tighter it squeezed.

"Shut your whimpering," he shouted at his wife. "As soon as I've dealt with this interfering pansy, you've got a lesson to learn." His lip curled as he looked her up and down. "And I'm gonna enjoy beating it into you." Her fingernails dug into the carpet underneath her as she looked down into her lap.

The ice in his voice sent a jolt through Lee's body and with a slight twist he managed to slip his thumb out from under the lasso.

His hand followed, allowing him to break free, but Jimmy was quick

to move, firing objects at him one after the other. As Lee showed no

visible ability yet, Jimmy seemed to gain in confidence as he tried

again to restrain him, but there was no denying that Lee was nimble.

He whipped his arm, sending the jet of light across the room and

around Lee's thigh, twisting up his body. Lee was pinned to the spot,

sweat breaking out in beads on his forehead and his eyes darting

around the room looking for a weapon, an escape, anything. Jimmy

slowly moved towards him, a vicious glint in his eye that said he was

used to getting his own way, eventually.

"This is a useful little weapon, isn't it? I find it particularly

useful for making people pay attention to me. In fact… I might hold

you there a little longer, so you get a front row view of the lesson I

have in store for Beth here." His body shuddered as if with laughter,

but no noise escaped his lips.

Seething with disgust and anger; every bone in his body, every

muscle fibre ached to get hold of this primitive tyrant. But as Jimmy

was delivering his speech, Lee had been working his phone free from its protective rubber covering, and held it in his hand waiting for the perfect moment. Jimmy's confidence grew as Beth's whimpers turned into sobs and he partially turned his back to Lee. He bent the rubber case around his hand, using it in a slicing motion, moving through the path of the electric lasso, cutting off its beam for a second, long enough for him to break his way out of its hold.

Before Jimmy had a chance to react, Lee had thrown himself on him, reigning down punches as he fell to the floor. He pinned him down with his knees and channelled all his anger into teaching this idiot a real lesson. As each punch landed he felt Jimmy weaken, until finally there was no resistance at all, yet still Lee's fist pummelled down into his face and chest. He moved his arms, one after the other, hearing and seeing nothing, not even the screams of Beth as she watched her abusive husband fall into unconsciousness.

His punches slowed and he raised his fist back to deliver another, only to see Beth's head and shoulders move into focus, bent over her husband's body. He paused for a second, seeing the light around her flicker as her protective force field went up, surrounding her. But it wasn't just her she was protecting; she was also surrounding her husband.

Lee's eyebrows knitted together as he blinked, trying to understand. Beth tentatively looked up, fear in her eyes as she waited to see what Lee would do next. His lips tried to form words, but he didn't know what to say. Instinctively he wanted to apologise, but this idiot deserved the beating. If he hadn't come upstairs, who knows what he would have done to Beth. But as he looked at her, cowering over her husband's limp figure, lying on the floor, the bruises already forming, he knew what she saw. He'd seen that look in people's eyes before. To her the devil she knew was a safer choice over the devil that was Lee.

All rage, anger and confidence drained from him with one exhaled breath. Feeling a deep sense of deflation and numbness Lee turned and made for the door. Passing through the doorway he reached down and gripped the handle. Pulling it from the ground and placing it in back in the frame he had kicked it from so violently moments before, leaving Beth and her abusive excuse of a husband to their privacy and to make the inevitable phone call to the cops to report what he had just done.

Walking down the stairs, opting not to return to his apartment, he left the building to seek a vantage point to await the influx of cops coming for him. Crossing the street Lee walked to the corner of the block where his favourite coffee shop was. Going inside, and sitting by the window he could see both up and down the entire block. There he quietly waited for either the waitress to come and take his order or for the cops to come and arrest him. Resigning himself to whichever came first, he knew it was out of his hands. He was, after all, powerless.

CHAPTER TWO

Teary eyed and irritated, Tom sat in the kitchen waiting for his father to return from the car. Unable to focus on the task before him, yet he continued to persevere. His eyes ached, forcing him to stop and clear the tears using the sleeve of his newly-bought shirt. Forgetting himself, he used his hand to clear the moisture from his eyes. This only made the pain worse.

Returning from the car with the brown paper bag in hand, Philip entered the kitchen. Taking one look at his son, a smile began to bend his lip. Through blurred vision Tom looked back at his father, and began to laugh heartily.

"You know how much I hate chopping onions."

Both men continued to laugh, Tom walking over to the sink, he grabbed a cloth and cleared his eyes. Philip took his place at the table and continued to chop.

"I know you hate chopping onions, but Lee loves them in his

birthday meal."

Philip had prepared every meal for his sons when they were kids and was accustomed to chopping onions and the stinging aroma did not bother him at all. Grabbing the big wooden spoon from beside the stove Tom took Philip's place at the big pot of bubbling sauce and began to stir.

Philip and Tom both knew Lee's struggle with his birthday and always tried to make it about him and not his mother. It was now a tradition that they would prepare a simple understated meal for all three of them. It was the only real tradition they still shared besides the obvious festive celebrations. Philip had his own tradition for this day, ever since the boys were young. Rising an hour before the rest of the house, he would quietly take his key and slip out. The boys never questioned what he did as they always knew. It was an uncomfortable reminder for Lee. Philip would come back a little emotional, but always with ingredients for both a good breakfast and Lee's favourite dinner. Lying in bed until the aroma of breakfast wafted through the house, the boys only arose when the sounds of plates hitting the table rang out. The breakfast tradition only ended when the boys moved out; Tom for basic training and Lee for college, but the custom of dinner lived on.

It dawned on Philip that he had forgotten one bag of groceries in the trunk. "Would you mind popping out and grabbing that last bag from the boot? I'll keep an eye on the sauce."

Tom replied. "No problem, just make sure it doesn't stick!" Philip, irritated by the comment, stated, "It's nearly thirty years I've been making this for your brother, and not once has it stuck. I don't intend on starting today."

Tom was a little taken aback by this but realised that as tough as this day was for Lee, it was always going to be a hell of a lot tougher for his Dad. So without snapping back he took the big spoon out of the pot, sitting it beside the oven once more and left the room.

Philip now finished chopping the onions and turned his knife to the carrots. Muttering to himself, "God sake Philip, it's not Toms fault. He's just trying to help." He knew he shouldn't have snapped at him for something so trivial. He began to think back to the real reason he was tetchy on this day.

On the day Lee was born, his parents had been coming home from the hospital, where his mum had been for her nine-month check-up. The day had been normal for the young couple, who were expecting their second child, having already had a boy two years before. Josephine dropped her husband to work in the hospital and went on to the school where she taught English.

At three thirty in the afternoon she finished up correcting the children's homework, putting away their projects at school and went to the hospital to have her scan. Meeting Philip in the reception he brought Josephine down the long corridor of maternity wards where they met the obstetrician. Dr. Cruz was a colleague of Philip's and looked after Josephine during her first pregnancy. As the doctor performed the scan Josephine's eyes were fixated on the screen as she held Philip's hand. Dr. Cruz made the image of the foetus clear on the screen and turned to Josephine, "Do you want to know the sex?"

Josephine hesitated. "No, I want it to be a surprise."

Turning to Philip she could see a huge smile on his face and she exclaimed. "Aw no fair, you can tell! Can't you?"

Philip simply chuckled, brushed his hand through her hair, kissed her on the head and told her, "We'll just have to wait and see." Getting their keepsake picture, they then left.

Philip drove, as his wife was tired, driving the same way home that he had done every day for the past five years. Some raindrops were still hitting the windscreen from an earlier downpour. Philip hit the wipers to clear any residual drops, muttering to himself, "I need to replace these wipers," as they weren't clearing the windscreen on the first wipe but rather taking at least three to clear his view. Josephine wasn't paying too much attention as they drove down the streets that felt like home, past the playground where they would walk Tom, their first child, in his pram.

She could vaguely recognize the sound of Philip's voice in the background, happily talking, but her mind was miles away. She was picturing her little girl or boy in her arms, sitting against the stomach that it now lay inside. She imagined pushing him or her down this road; chasing behind them as they learnt to walk; watching them carefully as her two children played together in the playground. In a matter of minutes, she had visualized the first decade of her unborn child's life. She thought about the friends they would make; the games they would play; the attitude they would have. Would it be a sunny happy child? A melancholy child, always fretting?

"So I sold the house and we're moving to Hawaii…" Philip looked across at Josephine, knowing exactly what she was thinking about and enjoying teasing her anyway.

"Hang on, what?!" she exclaimed, suddenly pulled out of her thoughts.

"You're miles away again. What is it this time? Dreaming of the unnatural musical ability he is bound to have?" he winked at her and briefly placed his hand on her leg, squeezing.

"Ha-ha, I'm sorry Philip. It's just… all the possibilities!" the twinkle in her eye that had appeared on that day all those months ago when she first told Philip that she was pregnant had only become brighter and stronger. She was a wonderful mother to Tom and he couldn't wait to see her with both children in her arms.

Pulling onto the highway they went to collect Tom from the childminder's. As they drove along the short stretch of road there was a large lorry carrying bulk metal in front of them.

Being a cautious man, he kept his distance as they drove. Looking ahead, Philip saw a small removal van, the kind used to move apartment furniture, join the highway and merge alongside the lorry. Approaching their exit, the removal van veered suddenly and violently in front of the lorry, as if to avoid something on the road. The warm smile that hadn't left Philip's face since they'd seen the scan vanished, replaced by intense concentration.

The van caused the lorry to jack-knife and it tipped onto its side. The horrendous noise of metal on metal and screeching tires was enough to send Josephine into a panicked hysteria, torn between clutching onto the door beside her and wrapping her arms around her unborn baby, but Philip was a meticulous man and had kept his distance. He had enough room to manoeuvre out of danger.

Unfortunately, the driver behind Philip wasn't as adept and careened into the back of his car, causing him to be thrust into the back of the lorry and allowing the bulk metal to rip apart the car and open it up like a cheap piece of tin. Philip had been knocked out.

*

Gradually starting to wake, feeling a combination of cold rain and warm blood cascading from his face, he found himself alone in the car. He could not see his beloved wife. He strained to get out of the car, eventually freeing himself from the seat and crawling out through the window. His hearing and vision had been impaired from the violent impact he'd taken to the head. All noise was inaudible, as if underwater, and his vision was blurred and fuzzy.

Struggling to his feet, he limped heavily on a badly damaged leg that had been twisted in the wreckage. Trying to put the full weight of his body on his leg, it simply couldn't take it and collapsed. Lying on the ground unable to move, shock was starting to set in. A horrible combination of burnt rubber, fuel and oil filled his nose. The scent acted like smelling salts and revived him. Feeling panicked he began to look for Josephine. Rolling onto his front he looked into the car, but she was not there. With quick stares his eyes darted all around, but he was unable to lay his eyes on her. The thought of his best friend and life partner alone, scared and quite possibly injured gripped onto his heart. And his child. His unborn child. Sweat dripped from his forehead as he frantically searched for them.

A moment of clarity hit him and he bolted to his feet, ignoring the pain that seared through his body like a hot poker on cold flesh. Dashing towards the rear of the car, he rounded the trunk, not noticing a loose piece of metal. Treading on it, it offered him no grip to the ground. Once again he collapsed as the smooth wet metal slid from under foot.

As he hit the ground, he could see round the side of the car to the passenger side. There she was, struggling to breathe, only managing to take short sharp breaths and struggling to cling onto consciousness. For a moment all he could do was stare at her, terrified of the reality of the situation. Labouring back to his feet, he went to tend to her. As he moved closer, the full extent of her injuries were hidden as she lay holding her open jacket across her chest.

"Are you okay, Joey?"

No words left her mouth and she simply pulled open her jacket. Philip's eyes widened, rising his hand to his mouth at the horror of what he was presented with. Sticking through her blood soaked blouse was a large piece of jagged metal puncturing her chest.

There was a large bend in the metal that Philip put straight with ease. Holding her gaze steady with his, he pulled the metal from her chest to free her from the wreckage. Josephine howled out in pain. Pulling the metal, he could feel the jagged edges rubbing, tearing against his wife's insides. The sound of Josephine shrieking and the feeling of his wife's bones on the metal were unbearable to him. Instead he tried to focus on the task at hand, saving the life of his wife and child. Biting back tears he looked down at her chest. The jagged metal left an open wound, but her ability to heal was drained by the later stages of pregnancy. There would be no way back from this. But he couldn't think of that. He couldn't face it. Putting pressure on the laceration he tried to stem the bleeding, all the while knowing in his heart that there was little hope for his beloved. Philip looked into the eyes of his wife and did something he had never done in all the years they were together. He lied. She looked up at him and struggled to speak.

Philip reassuringly spoke to her in hushed tones. "It's ok, you are going to be fine, you need to save your strength."

Knowing she was hearing lies and choosing to ignore the comfort Philip was offering, she continued to struggle painfully for speech. Words she searched for would not come easily given the extent of her trauma; she kept trying and eventually forced out the words, "Save my baby."

Looking into the back seat of the car, Philip reached for his medical bag. Right there in the middle of all that devastation, disarray and through immeasurable heartache, h e performed a procedure that had not been done for an age. Taking his scalpel, he cut into his wife. As he cut her open a combination of amniotic fluid and blood poured out. Reaching his hand into her open womb he removed their child. Quickly he pulled off his coat and wrapped it around the newborn child. Teary eyed, devastated and completely numb from shock, he placed the child in his dying wife's arms. Through his pain he struggled to say, "Look Joey, it's our little boy."

Unable to lift her arms to offer her son a cuddle, Josephine simply lay with her son propped up on her dying body, unable to move an inch. Looking at her son for the first time with fading eyes, she pushed out one more word.

"Lee."

Breaking down, Philip kissed her softly on the lips. As a tear rolled down her cheek she gave one last breath and with that, she died on the side of the road amid all that chaos. Philip was left to deal with the devastation that followed this tragic event. Every morning he woke up to the heartache of knowing the loss of the one person who filled his heart; the only woman he truly loved, the person he expected to grow old with. And as much as he wanted to lie in bed all day, going through photo albums and thinking over moments long since passed with his beloved Joey, he was not able to wallow in this pain, having two young boys to raise and provide for.

Over the coming years he did just that, moving past his own pain and focusing on the two people most important in the entire world to him. He was a caring father who taught his boys the importance of being good and just. At times he was a little hard and strict with his boys, but he always had their best interests at heart.

*

Tom returned from the car with the bag in hand. Seeing his father sitting at the table appearing to be uncharacteristically emotional, he entered and took the knife from his hand. He sat in the chair beside him and began to chop. Philip stood up and went to the oven, lifting the wooden spoon once again and plunging it into the pot. After a couple of stirs he began to laugh.

"What's up?" Tom asked quizzically from the table.

"I guess there's a first for everything," Philip proclaimed. The sauce is sticking!" Once again both men laughed.

Tom gathered up all the onions and carrots and dropping them into the pot, told his father, "Don't worry, you know Lee. He'll never notice and if he does he won't say anything."

CHAPTER THREE

The inevitable wailing of sirens he had expected hadn't come and he was unsure if they would. Were he in Jimmy's position he knew without doubt that he would have reported it. But he wasn't Jimmy.

Beginning to relax, Lee turned his eyes downward to the coffee cup clasped tightly in his hand. What remained of the heat that emanated out from the drink was fading fast, but this didn't seem to bother him, as he slowly sipped on the now lukewarm cappuccino, enjoying the cool froth as he got closer to the bottom of the cup. He contemplated going to the counter to order another, but the option to just sit and reflect won out.

Today was always bittersweet. Well, more bitter than sweet. Every year this day would roll by and he would face an internal rift that weighed heavily on him. Mostly he spent it thinking about his family and hiding the fact that it was meant to be a joyous occasion rather than a sombre one, but for him every year brought with it a small feeling of guilt, a feeling that if today was not his birthday his life might have been very different.

Lee thought back on the life his parents had; it was a life that he could barely imagine, in comparison to his own. But no, it wasn't so much the life that he envied, but the love they shared. Philip and Josephine had been high school sweethearts and had only known love for each other. Josephine was free-spirited with a kind heart and a soft soul that reflected in her outlook on life. She would often be seen tending her garden or painting outside, if the mood took her. She had no illusions of grandeur; she was humble, loving and lived for her family. Philip, in contrast, had quite a regimental upbringing. His father had been a soldier in the war whose special skill was covert sabotage missions, often finding himself behind enemy lines for most of the duration of the war. These skills he imparted onto his son, taking him hunting high in the woods for days at a time, teaching him how to remain concealed amongst the natural environment and how to conceal his scent using the wind and read the land around him.

Lee spent his younger years listening to his father talk

about his grandfather, a man Lee never met but one who would shape his life through the teachings he bestowed upon Philip. Lee listened to his father with a respect that shone through his eyes.

"When I wasn't out hunting with your granddad, I was learning mechanical skills in the old shed behind the main house. Now it's a broken down old building, but then it was magnificent. Everything was shiny and all his tools were kept in such order that he could always lay his hand on the tool he was looking for. We spent summer after summer mostly by taking apart pre-war vehicles and restoring them to their former glory." He paused as his eyes stared ahead, reliving those moments of simplistic joy. "After your granddad died, and I set about working on an engine, I could then - and still can - hear his voice guiding my hand and telling me what to do."

Philip's father had seen the horrors of war and although he didn't want that life for his son, he appreciated that the balance of power was on such a knife-edge that if a war were to flare again, he would want him to be as prepared as possible.

Even though his father was stern towards him and expected a lot from him, he always knew he loved him, even if he had difficulty showing it. Philip chose a selfless life, helping others by becoming a doctor and it was this choice that showed his father he had raised a good man.

His parents seemed polar opposites in many respects, but as a couple they just seemed to work. Their contrasting personalities appeared to balance, shaping the perfect relationship. They had their ups and downs as many young couples did, but both knew that love wasn't about perfection, but rather it was about compromise. The mutual respect that they had for each other was unwavering and while the heady romance of their youth had settled down to a simmering glow, their mutual respect and admiration meant that they each would happily compromise for the other. They were a sensible couple, who worked hard in their youth to be in a position to start a family and be able to provide a good life for their future.

Lee paused his thoughts and looked down at his hands. His unfinished coffee sat between them and now leant a pale stain to the inside of his cup. He stared down at it as he swirled the inch of liquid around the cup, a heavy sense of melancholy sitting on his shoulders. He thought back further, to a time before his parents were born and even before his granddad was born. Reminiscing on a time where he would have fitted into the world quite normally; a time where evolution wouldn't have been so cruel as to make him feel alone in the world; the only ordinary man in a world of power.

Today's world was very different to the one that Lee dreamt off. And dream he often did. Although practical and hard working by nature, there was something hollow inside him; a feeling that he didn't belong, and try as he might, he couldn't escape this weighty feeling. So he consoled himself with his own thoughts of a world long since gone and the opposite of everything he now lived with. But those dreams always ended too quickly, leaving him with the reality of this life, where everyone is special, where the ability to do incredible things is an everyday occurrence and each person is gifted with an ability beyond the realm of what is comparable. In this world a child might have the ability to throw a car through the air; a person does not necessarily need a plane for the ability to fly; the most difficult mathematical problems can be solved in a matter of seconds by high school students.

In this world, evolution took a major leap forward, unlocking the full potential of the human mind. This potential manifests itself differently in every being on this planet, gifting people with powers, an inherent concealed ability that manifests itself either through a physical capability or a mental ability. With these abilities there are a few effects on the human body, like physical exhaustion. It is easy to exhaust one's power; the veiled capability of an individual tends to last about an hour or so. After a prolonged splurge of hidden virtue, an individual is left weakened, drained and in need of rest; thus for every person's strength there is a corresponding weakness as unique to the individual as their abilities.

This is a world that knows only peace. There are no crimes of any significance other than basic crimes any good beat cop could handle; no wars at all. This is a world where good and evil co-exist and have found equilibrium for survival, but this was not always the case. Crime tried to take over, with evil trying to take advantage of newfound strengths. People could simply walk into banks and take money, should they choose to.

People who choose to murder and rape can never be seen committing crimes. Power-hungry leaders waged wars against weaker countries to steal natural resources and enslave the people as victims of war. Good people had to rise up against tyranny and a world war was fought.

A young boy stood back from the table behind Lee, scraping his chair noisily along the floor as he did so, waking Lee from his reverie. He licked his lips and rolled his shoulders back, once more taking note of his surroundings. People going about their business in the normal way and yet none of them were normal. You could never tell what any one individual's strength or weakness would be, although that did work to Lee's advantage. He considered each person in the little café he sat in, imagining what their strength could be and how it might affect their day-to-day life. Did anyone else long for a different life as he did? He sighed; looking down at his hands clenched together so tightly the whites of his knuckles glared at him. Slowly he released them, letting the frustration out through his nose. He needed to pull himself together and get on with his day. Yet something stopped him. The desire to carry on and pretend that he didn't want something more, something that his parents always had, just wasn't there. A flicker of shame settled in his stomach as he admitted to himself that just this once he wanted to wallow a little longer, his mind taking him back to a point where his father began to realise Lee was different.

Being a single father with a full-time job didn't make things easy. His two sons were both regular boys, they were fanatical about sports and would sit together and watch football and wrestling on the TV, often acting out the moves of their favourite wrestlers. Philip would take the boys out for food on the nights where his long hours got the better of him, leaving him reluctant to face the arduous task of cleaning up after dinner, although he actually enjoyed cooking for the boys.

To Lee and Tom this was a welcome treat as Philip only ever had healthy food in the house and the idea of getting a burger and milkshake always seemed like such an exciting prospect. Philip would always allow Lee to order first, turning to him and asking, "What looks good Lee?" But no matter where they went for food, Lee would always look to his brother for guidance saying, "I don't really know, Dad. What you think Tom?" and nearly always Lee would ask for the same as Tom, unless there were mushrooms in it. Lee hated mushrooms and Tom loved them, often ordering extra mushrooms to goad a reaction from Lee.

They fought like normal boys do and had a textbook relationship. When Lee turned ten, his father became aware that he didn't seem to have developed any of his hidden abilities yet. By is twelfth birthday he had still shown no heightened ability and his father grew concerned. He kept a close eye on him and subtly tested him by asking him to do things he couldn't. Testing his strength, he would ask him to lift a box that he had deliberately weighted down. Or when he cut his leg he observed the wound, noticing that he had no accelerated healing. These were the most likely powers for him to have, as they were the powers his parents had. Philip began to see powers in everything he did, hoping to himself that each time he saw something it would be his power.

Philip took Lee and Tom to the local fair and as they strolled along the stalls looking at all the various games and rides, Lee freed his hand from his father's. Philip did not notice this as his eyes were gazing up to the big wheel. Excited at the prospect of taking his kids on the ride he turned and said, "What do you think boys? Are you game?" But when he looked down only Tom was standing there looking at him. Philip exclaimed, "Where's Lee!"

Tom quickly looked around, not seeing his brother he simply shrugged his shoulders. Philip grabbed Tom's hand and ran back the way they came. If Tom hadn't had the same ability as Philip he may have broken his arm, but with Tom's strength it just felt like Philip was gripping him a little firmer than usual.

Philip didn't have to go too far to find Lee; he came upon a dark stall with the small solitary figure of Lee standing in front of it; the only person giving it any attention. Philip was relieved to see his son safe and became aware of the pressure he was putting on Tom's hand. He loosened his grip and fell to his knee to make sure he hadn't hurt Tom. After a quick examination he knew Tom was fine.

Philip approached Lee, saying sternly "Lee!"

But Lee did not turn.

Philip said again "Lee?" this time placing his hand on the young boy's shoulder. The boy moved his head but did not break his eyes away from what his gaze was fixated upon.

Lee simply said, "Ten thousand, one hundred and eighty-seven." Philip did not understand what his son was saying until he looked into the stand and saw a giant glass container full of jellybeans with a sign over it saying 'Guess the amount, Win the Prize'.

"Ten thousand, one hundred and eighty-seven," Lee repeated again.

Philip's heart skipped as he reached his hand into his pocket and pulled out some money so Lee could register his guess and handed it to the woman in the stall.

"How much do you think is in it?" the woman asked Lee.

Once again Lee said, "Ten thousand, one hundred and eighty-seven."

The woman's face was overcome with surprise. "Aren't you a clever boy!" She reached for a giant teddy and she handed it to Lee.

Philip took the boys up the big wheel and while the landscape stretched before him, captivating his boys, he could not enjoy the view. He didn't gaze at the stars as his wide-eyed sons did. Instead he was fixated on *ten thousand, one hundred and eighty-seven* and hoped to himself that he had finally discovered his son's ability.

Packing the boys into the car, he watched in amazement as his little son dragged the teddy bear that was twice his size into the back seat with him and carefully fastened the spare seatbelt around the bear, while Tom hopped into the front.

They were heading home when Philip pulled the car into a gas station to buy some things. The boys thought they were in for a treat when their Dad arrived back with seven large boxes of cereal, something he would never ordinarily allow them to have. When they arrived home Philip sent the boys into the house. Staying behind in the garage, they could hear him tearing the boxes open and pouring the cereal out.

The boys waited by the door and their curiosity spiked. Philip called out, "Lee," and the two boys entered. Philip looked up at them coming in the door.

"Now Lee, have a look at this…" revealing a large glass vase full to the top with a mixture of the different cereals. "Lee, how much is in the vase?"

He automatically looked to Tom for his input, but before his eyes met Tom's, Philip interrupted him.

"Lee, take your time and tell me what you think."

He stared at the container and after a moment he stated,

"Eight thousand, six hundred and twelve."

Philip's mouth curved with a smile. "Right, now boys, time for bed." They did as their father asked and they left the room. Philip waited for them to go and then set about counting the contents of the container.

Lee and Tom lay in their beds chatting about what had happened. Lee was hopeful, asking Tom, "What do you think? Do you think I was right?"

"I don't know, Lee," Tom replied. "I suppose we will find out tomorrow."

After all the excitement of the day the boys soon fell asleep. When they awoke they both ran downstairs to find a very tired Philip at the kitchen table sitting over a coffee. Looking at their father without saying anything he could read the question in Lee's eyes and all he said was, "Not even close." He laughed to himself at the ludicrousness of the test he had just performed.

Lee's heart broke as he felt pulled back out of a world he

wanted to be accepted into. Sadness set in as he sat thinking he would never have an answer to the question. Philip was surprised by this, seeing the sadness in his little son and decided enough was enough. He could not subtly test him anymore, as his son was becoming aware that he was different. He could no longer waste time taking him to the hospital where he worked and running a barrage of tests to determine if there was anything wrong with his son. All the tests had come back normal. He was a normal happy twelve-year-old boy, but with one big difference. In a world where the norm is to be different, being less than normal was too hard for a boy of his age to comprehend and deal with.

Philip determined that it would be best for Lee and Tom if no one found out that Lee was different, all the while hoping that Lee was just a late developer. Philip was afraid that if anyone found out that Lee had no ability he would be taken away from him and barbaric experiments would be performed on him. The same experiments that the governments of the past were guilty of. Afraid that his son would be hailed as a missing link from this time to a world that had long passed, he decided to protect his boys. He would have to put a plan into action.

Given Philip's background he was in a position where he could impart onto his sons the skills and lessons his father taught him all those years ago. So from the time Lee was twelve his father trained him; having super strength was a bonus. He started Lee on a fitness routine that he would stick with for the majority of his life, involving daily runs of five miles, two hundred press ups each morning and night, accompanied by the very healthy diet he had always instilled, being a doctor. He trained him to become a skilful fighter through many ancient arts of combat. Most importantly, he instilled the values of what he felt it meant to be a man; the values of honour, discipline, dignity, selflessness and self-reliance.

His brother Tom developed strength just like his father, so physically he didn't need the routine that his brother did, but they would often spar together as kids, Lee learning how to use his brother's momentum and strength against him. Philip decided to educate both his boys, teaching them about the world, about the past and the present, teaching them right from wrong, and giving them the tools to develop terrific minds.

He taught the young boys how to solve equations, puzzles and all about the outdoors; how to track and hunt, how to read the land around them so that they could look at the stars and know exactly where they were and where they had to go. No matter how lost Lee and Tom would be, they would always know which direction to turn, just as Philip's father had taught him.

Philip was at work one day when he got a call from the boys' school asking him to come in, that there had been an incident involving his sons. Automatically Philip assumed that Lee's secret had been found out. Alarmed by this, he grabbed his coat and darted straight out the door. Philip didn't mind running out on his patients for his boys as they were his main priority in life; however, the patient that Philip was in the middle of giving a hernia examination to wasn't as amused by the situation, being left behind in the examination room with only his gown to cover his embarrassment.

Making haste, he got to the school and went straight to the office. Sitting outside he found his two sons, each of whom saw him come in, but neither were brave enough to look him in the eye. Philip automatically knew the boys were guilty of something. He entered the principal's office and sat down. The principal, Mr. Pine, greeted Philip at the door with a firm handshake.

"Thanks for coming so soon, Mr. Sapota. Please have a seat."

Sitting down, Philip's fears that Lee had been found out ran through his mind in double time, but he was smart enough to let the principle speak first.

"Mr. Sapota, there are certain things we as teachers can observe. Over time these observations lend themselves to conclusions. For example, having Tom in the school these past few years, it is fairly easy to tell within reason what his ability is."

Philip stood up as anxiety hit. Mr Pine continued. "Don't worry Mr Sapota; this is the same for all the kids who pass through these corridors. In fact, there are very few students who pass these halls that I don't get an indication of their gift." Hearing this Philip relaxed and sat back in his chair allowing him to continue.

"Lee is one of those students, for whatever reason his gift has never been..."

Philip interrupted the principal, growing impatient. "Mr Pine. Enough of this circling the issue. Can you tell me why I'm here?"

Standing up and walking to the window, Mr Pine spoke. "Mr Sapota, today at break a bunch of older kids started picking on Tom. Name-calling, the usual kind of thing. But don't worry, I will be speaking to their parents as well."

Philip was now paying full attention to the principal, heeding his words more intently than before, knowing Tom to be more than capable of physically looking after himself.

"Now the problem wasn't Tom or what was being said to him. In fact, Tom was highly restrained, given my past observations. The reason I called you in, is Lee and how he reacted."

Without realizing it, Philip slipped forward in his seat

becoming engrossed in the words the principle was speaking.

"Lee saw what was happening to his brother and he did not show the same restraint that Tom did."

Mr Pine hesitated as if to consider the best way to tell Philip what had happened. "Basically Mr Sapota, Lee beat up three students. Not only three students, but they are three of the biggest kids in the school, and two of them are powerful, very powerful. Lee managed to do this without revealing his own ability. I saw this with my own eyes. Now Mr Sapota, I have seen kids pass through these doors for years and I have never seen a child move with this mixture of physical self-awareness and rage. It's clear that your son has been trained physically. Emotionally, I am not so sure!"

Philip took heed of what Mr Pine said, reassuring him that it would not happen again before motioning to leave his office. "If it's okay with you I'd like to take the boys home. I need to have a talk with them."

CHAPTER FOUR

Philip thought that maybe the reason Lee was so angry and apart from the world was because he didn't understand it. He wanted Lee and Tom to know where they came from. He wanted them to know the history of the world and how it came to be today. Sitting them down he instilled the knowledge of the world as best he could, hoping not to show any personal bias so the boys could come to their own conclusion on the state of the world.

He began with the leap itself, taking a deep breath as he started on the voyage of discovery with his two boys, biting back the pain that stabbed at his heart, at the thought of his beautiful Josephine missing the experience.

"Now boys, I am going to throw a lot of information at you and if you are finding it hard to understand please make sure you let me know, as it is important for you to understand this.

There is no real point in going too far before the leap as that history is now irrelevant, so to speak and is seen as ancient, so we will begin with the leap. It was my grandparents' generation who were the first to feel the full effects of this leap in evolution. Before that, only about forty percent of the population was affected. This leap in evolution came about when children started taking longer to develop in the womb; it began to take an additional 3 months for a child to develop.

It is said that in the last three months of pregnancy a child would develop their abilities. Initial testing on babies who took longer to be born was inconclusive, as the abilities the children held only manifested in early adolescence. It was only a few years later that people began to understand there was something very different about these children. Stories began to leak out about children with exceptional abilities performing extraordinary feats. The people performing these feats became known as the Gifted Generation.

Panic ensued; many of the children were taken from their parents for experimentation, but all these experiments proved to be fruitless. These youngsters were biologically identical to kids with no special abilities; Governments experimented on the kids to test the boundaries of their abilities. Exhausting their abilities then performing invasive tests, both physically and psychologically."

Hearing this Lee broke the spell that held him and Tom and spoke up. "What kind of tests?"

"Most of the testing was done in secret facilities far away from the eyes of society. I don't really know exactly what they did but the few people who managed to escape these facilities spoke of human rights atrocities."

Philip knew exactly what tests were performed but didn't want to cause his son distress. As he feared that if found out those same tests would be performed on him. So he steered the conversation away from the past atrocities perpetrated by previous barbaric governments. This is where the soothing words of his beloved Josephine would really have helped. He longed for her reassuring touch on his shoulder as he continued on with the lesson.

"Many parents who had children of the gifted generation taught their children never to reveal their dynamism as they might be taken away from them, experimented on and they would not be able to protect them.

Initially, the children romanticised their abilities and considered themselves super heroes, living selflessly. Dressing up in costumes to hide their identity, they tried to make the world a better place, a safer place. As they matured into adults, however, many of them had their view of the world they lived in twisted by things they saw.

It was not only the testing done on the fellow members of the gifted generation, but what people in positions of authority had done to get their power and maintain it. Like the misappropriation of wealth, the corruption in the banking system, the lack of humanity shown to the poorer people in the world. It was these injustices that led a lot of the gifted generation to become highly self-aware. They were of the opinion that if a group of people as a collective can't look out for each other, then why should an individual be expected to.

A few among the gifted generation began to justify breaking the law for their own financial gain. They would rationalise robbing a bank with the comment that 'the bank has robbed us for long enough.' Crime levels escalated; criminals always justifying their actions and their own flawed moral standpoint. Even as the number of gifted individuals grew, the governments of the time began to recruit these individuals, firstly to protect their own lands, later to ward off attacks from other governments and inevitably to launch such attacks themselves, all the while smugly justifying their actions and claiming they were 'to protect the sovereignty' of their respective nations. It wasn't long until such acts escalated and almost the entire world became embroiled in war.

As you know, my Dad, your granddad was a soldier, but not by choice. He wasn't conscripted or anything but rather he felt duty bound."

The two boys began to listen more intently as they rarely heard Philip talk about their granddad's role in the war.

"Your granddad specialised in sabotage missions. This meant that rather than killing people in the war he in actuality risked his life to save those around him. He would sneak behind enemy lines and sabotage the heavy artillery that would cause so much havoc, often undertaking missions that others would refuse as they were seen as suicidal. Actually on one occasion a squadron was pinned down and surrounded in a large wooded area. It was the depths of winter and they were running out of supplies and on the verge of starvation. Your granddad was under strict orders not to attempt a rescue, but feeling duty bound to the men, he did exactly the opposite. In one night my Dad, your granddad went behind enemy lines and using the cover of night he sabotaged four heavy artillery guns, two tanks and…" choosing his words carefully so that he didn't scare the boys he continued "…neutralised countless infantry. He did all this virtually unarmed and undetected. Making his way to the troops that were pinned down." Philip's face started to show pride as he told the boys the outcome. "In one night he saved forty-eight soldiers. Taking no credit for his actions he swore each one of them to silence, so as not to make his presence known to his superiors. Each man he saved won the medal of valour for their bravery in the face of an insurmountable force and were allowed go home. If not for my Dad, they all would have been going home anyway but each would have been draped in a flag and to the tune of a lonely fife player."

Philip walked over to the cabinet by the fireplace and reaching his hand into the back of the top shelf he pulled out an old tin tobacco box that was rusty around the side. It rattled in his hand as he took it down as if it was full of coins. Handing it to Tom he opened it and looked inside. "After the war this was sent to your granddad and he kept it. Each offering a testament to his bravery."

Tom opened the box and Lee stood over his shoulder and peered into it. The rusty box opened and the boys could see heaped together covered in fine dust, forty-eight medals, each a token representing a life saved. They looked up into each other's eyes at the same moment, each boy speechless as the weight of this reality rested in their hands.

"Your Granddad often wondered what became of the men after the war, but was content with knowing that because of him they survived it and each of them knew why."

Philip broke his lesson, checking with the boys that they understood what he was teaching them. He asked them questions to make sure all the information he was throwing at them, although complex, was being absorbed. When he was happy that the boys understood what they were being told he moved the conversation away from his father's role in the war and went on to explain the policy history that in turn caused the war. It was in teaching the boys about the war that he revealed his true opinions on world politics.

"The war was very basic in its composition. There were two global factions, each representing one of the world's two superpowers; the old faction and the new. You know these factions as The Old World Alliance and The United New World. The United New World faction preached that all men were free and were to be treated so, irrespective of whether a person had an ability or not, the Old World Alliance faction had a policy of embracing the evolutionary leap to further the human development.

Nations aligned themselves accordingly with their government policies. There was a third class of countries, neutral in all matters. These countries did not adopt a new name for their alliance, but maintained neutrality.

The Old World Alliance outwardly had a policy of treating all individuals the same. The appropriation of wealth was to be divided out equally between the inhabitants of countries allied to their cause. People who lived in the countries of The Old World Alliance were told that they were living in paradise and given propaganda touting the evils that lay in The United New World.

The Old World Alliance preached that the people in the lands of their foe were living under a corrupt and a moralistic regime, rife with crime, and did not know what freedom was or what it meant to be free.

The Government of the Old World Alliance ruled with an iron fist and was to be obeyed at all times. Anyone who openly questioned the government was interned and never heard from again. Everyday crime was low here, as the atrocities inflicted on the citizens were not seen as crime, but law. Large criminal gangs had influence on the streets and with certain members of the Old World Alliance. The alliance used people with abilities to create a super-human army and used the threat of war against anyone who stood in their way.

In contrast, The United New World actually employed the freedoms that were preached by its adversary, creating a capitalist policy in terms of economic matters. This created a very clear and evident class system, where the rich would only get richer and the poor would get poorer.

If a person were to look at how The United New World applied policies, it would seem the perfect system, but a person delving deeper could see how these policies affected the lower and middle classes; these people might take another point of view. As the United New World allowed people to protect their abilities, they did not have the military strength that their archenemies had. What they lacked in military manpower, they made up for in economic terms.

Through education and self-advancement, the people were of superior intellect and were much stronger financially. This meant they had fewer soldiers who embraced their powers for the purposes of war. They were able to rectify the gap through investing in technology that would level the military playing field."

Philip paused again, allowing the boys a moment to take it all in and considering the weight of the information himself. He thought over what was being said to the boys and thought that his views were a reflection of the idolisation of his own father, considering how he was moulded by the war and the things he had seen and how in turn that affected Philip's own development; making him seemingly distant from outward emotion. Composing himself, he tried to stick to the black and white of what happened; at least his own interpretation of it.

"It is hard for anyone to remember who fired the first shot in the war, but both sides knew that the conflict itself was inevitable. The war started as many do; a war of economy.

The United New World first imposed sanctions upon the countries that aligned themselves with The Old World Alliance. They would trade only with themselves and neutral countries.

It was strongly favoured that neutral countries only trade with the United New World, to which most did as they saw The Old World Alliance to be too authoritarian and brutal towards its own people. These sanctions allowed the United New World to grow in prosperity and become the predominant world power.

Smaller members of the Old World Alliance saw prosperity in the polices that were being adopted in neighbouring countries, allowing for better infrastructure, health care, education and economic growth.

These smaller members did not see why they were handing over their nation's resources to be dictatorially ruled. Some of these countries reached out to The United New World to ask to help to break the chains of tyranny imposed by the Old World Alliance.

The United New World had a policy of helping smaller countries to move away from the Old World Alliance's control and to align them with their own viewpoint. However, these policies would only be fully enacted if the country that wanted to realign itself had large, if not substantial, natural resources that could then be traded to the United New World as a dowry for freeing them.

As countries began to move away, The Old World Alliance tightened control on smaller member states and engaged in mass propaganda to maintain power. Events escalated and eventually the economic war evolved into all-out war.

This was a war that neither side could win, nor could afford to lose. War raged for an age; each side cancelled out the other, as the abilities of one side was countered. After fourteen years of fighting and destruction, a truce was d r a w n up, and from that time to this, the world has known only peace.

As the next generation of children grew up, it became clear that they all would benefit from the leap in evolution and that all the kids had developed an ability of some sort. This generation also grew up knowing only war and it was this knowledge that led to the signing of the peace treaty.

The treaty forced The Old World alliance to improve their human rights policies and discontinue any desecration of the human form in the name of advancing the human race. The treaty also enacted policies by which the United New World would trade openly with the Old World Alliance to increase the balance of economic wealth and prosperity. Both sides opened their borders and allowed relatively free movement between the two government's controlled areas. The treaty held the balance of power between governments and the power that they shared was finite, to say the very least. This balance of peace would hold true over the next two generations, right up to the current day."

Philip stopped there, feeling that maybe all this information thrown at the two young boys might have been lost on them. He let out a sigh, releasing the pressure that had built up as he delivered this information and told them to go outside and play, which they were both happy to do.

Throughout the conversation Philip thought that to some extent Tom was unable to absorb that quantity of information, as his attention shifted from his father to gazing out of the window. Lee, on the other hand, absorbed it like a sponge, hanging on his every word as if searching for answers to questions he was asking himself about his own shortcomings.

Later that evening Philip returned to the topic with the boys, gently quizzing them to find out how much they had taken in. It was clear from the outset that Lee had an astonishing appetite for information and ability to recall it, as Lee was able to divulge back to him in great detail everything that he was taught by his father. This, Philip hoped, might have been his power, but Lee wasn't so fortunate.

*

Lee brought his attention to the cold cup in front of him

and pushed it to one side with irritation, as the real reason for his birthday melancholy came to mind once more. Every year he couldn't help but recall his own history to mind, as if by retelling himself his own story it could change a past that haunted him. He went through it in his mind systematically, with an eerie detachment that never lasted long enough. He tried to put himself in his father's shoes as he considered how he felt knowing a second son was about to be born, but it was near impossible. Imagining that kind of connection with someone, bringing new life into the world. A life that was completely and utterly your responsibility. A life that you would have to love, no matter what problems it caused, who it hurt, who's life it turned upside down.

The distant sound of sirens pulled Lee from his deep thoughts. Hearing sirens ringing out and bracing himself for the inevitable, only to see a fire engine whizz past the coffee shop on the other side and not even turn onto his block. Looking at his watch confused and thinking, *why aren't the cops here?* Maybe Jimmy was afraid to call the cops as he would have to explain a lot more than just bruises on himself. Most certainly the cops would question the bruises on Beth.

Content that he was not going to have to call his father from a jail cell, he picked himself up and went to his family.

CHAPTER FIVE

Lee joined Tom and Philip for dinner; it was always a welcome relief to him to have them close at hand. Only when he was sitting in a room with them did he have a feeling of belonging, a sense of acceptance that had never been easy for him to come by in the outside world.

After the dinner was finished Philip disappeared for his post dinner ritual of two laps of the block and, unbeknownst to his boys, a sneaky cigarette when no one was looking.

Lee busied himself by the sink, working his way through the pile of dishes. Tom walked into the room from the sitting room where he had been rattling through his bags.

Placing a box on the sink beside Lee, he turned to sit at the table without talking. Lee spied the box and asked, "What's this?"

Tom laughed, "Oh, I forgot you don't have x-ray vision,

open and you will see!"

Lee looked at Tom not knowing if he should be insulted, but before he had time to say anything Tom hastened him, "Go on!"

Quickly drying his hands, Lee lifted the box and sat at the table opposite Tom. Opening the box to see a dull blade inside, Tom interrupted the process and asked, "Do you recognise that?" Seeing the handle on the old knife Lee knew straight away exactly what was in front of him.

"Only you, Tom, could make a great present out of something I already own!" Taking the knife in his hand and removing it from the box be continued. "Man I haven't seen this thing in years. Where did you find it?"

"I have me ways," Tom stated and as his brother inspected the knife Tom went on. "Do you remember that day?"

"How could I forget, I was a kid and you nearly got me killed." Lee replied.

Tom acknowledged "Well, if Dad ever knew I think

both of us would have been."

The incident had happened many years before; Philip bought a cabin high in the mountains, keeping it a secret from everyone except his two sons. This was the place where he would take his boys at the weekends and holidays to train and study. It was also a sanctuary to Philip, a place to go to escape the world after his wife passed. Often going for long hikes himself, he could regularly be found there working on reconditioning vintage muscle cars; buying wrecked cars and totally rebuilding them as he did with his father all those years previously, never keeping them for too long, only long enough to find his next project.

The education given to Lee would also benefit his brother as the two boys were always at each other's side. One of the most important things Philip instilled in his sons was the importance of going unseen, both as a survival tactic and also as an everyday tool to be applied to his life. Philip taught the two boys to use and trust their instincts, ingraining a mantra into their subconscious; "Trust your gut. It won't lie to you. If something doesn't feel right, it's wrong."

Philip also taught Lee that he was different, special, and if anyone other than his brother found out, this could put himself and Tom in danger; fearing that if the truth got out Lee could be taken away from them and tested as if he were a Neanderthal in a world of homo sapiens, a link to a forgotten past.

Needing to know if the training regime the boys were on was actually working, Philip brought the boys high up into the mountains and gave them limited supplies.

He handed them some hunting and tracking gear and looked them dead in the eye as he spoke to them. "It will take you four days to get off this mountain safely; I have given you enough water for two days and equipment to catch your own food. I have installed a GPS tracking tag into each of your coats and an emergency beacon, so if you do get in trouble, activate it and I will come and get you. You are to set up camp here for tonight and start to make your way off the mountain and back to the cabin in the morning..."

Once again he reminded his sons, "Trust your gut. It

won't lie to you. If something doesn't feel right, it's wrong," and with that Philip left.

The two boys sat down and began to plan their route off the mountain; they decided that contrary to their father's wishes they would in fact set off that evening rather than wait for the next day.

They were keen to impress their father, determined to navigate the four-day trail in two days. Thinking this would evoke feelings of pride in their sometimes- d i s t a n t father. Lee hoped with this opportunity he would prove himself to his father as equal to everyone else in the world and that maybe with his approval on this Philip might stop treating him as an outcast, different to everyone else, and his shortcomings would no longer become an issue to Philip and to himself.

They were above the snow line and wanted to get below it before considering camping down for the night. Reaching the edge of the snowline darkness set in and the boys considered stopping, but both were too keen to continue. They sat down to change their socks, which by now were wet from the deep snow spilling over the tops of their boots. As Lee slipped off his boots Tom snickered looking at the socks that were on his feet. Lee looked at him, slightly agitated by Tom's guffaw. He barked, "What are you laughing at?"

Tom pointed to the water-soaked socks on his brother's feet. Lee, looking at his feet, couldn't help but smile as he had unwittingly worn Kermit socks for the hike. Lee laughed back good-naturedly. "Well, at least they are my lucky socks."

Tom reached into his pack and pulled out a thick pair of green thermal army socks, handing them to him with a grin. "I think these might be a little better suited."

Lee pulled on his brother's socks, tied up his boots and began to traverse the mountain. Guided by the stars, they navigated through the woodland with only the moonlight to illuminate their path. Walking most of the night, they stopped only for three hours, when the night was at its darkest, to rest. Finding cover at the foot of a ridge protected from the wind and under the cover of thick foliage they bedded down for a while.

They arose before dawn and packed away all their equipment and were ready to continue on their way. There were no complications the first day; understanding exactly what to do and where they needed to go. They needed to walk ten hours and then find shelter, allowing two hours for respite and route re-adjustment, correcting any navigational errors they made along the way. While walking they needed to find a water source and a source of food. They found the water easily and decided to source food when they found the best place to bed down.

By the time night began to fall on the second night the two boys were setting up camp in what seemed like a sleepy wooded area. They found a spot where they would be sheltered from the wind and rain and started to make camp.

Setting a snare at a rabbit hole in the hope it would provide them with dinner, Tom waited nearby to see if his endeavour would prove fruitful. Lee sat by the fire, poking life into it when he heard a high-pitched yelp. A flicker of remorse set in, knowing what the screech meant. Waiting for the return of his brother he grew impatient, wondering why he was taking so long to reappear with the food. Lee walked in the direction the noise had come from, and after a few minutes he came across his brother on his knees. Lee, approaching from behind, was able to peer over Tom's shoulder and saw tangled up in the snare was a beautiful snowy coloured rabbit.

Tom didn't turn but could hear his brother behind him. With his eyes fixated on the rabbit all he could muster was, "I can't do it."

Lee answered, "It's suffering, you have to."

Tom bowed his head a little lower. "I know, but I can't."

The rabbit tried to kick its legs to get away but the strain only tightened the snare around its neck, cutting in further. Witnessing this, Lee reached across his brother's shoulder and took hold of the rabbit. Lifting it, he gripped the rabbit around the neck and squeezed tightly. The rabbit twitched to loosen his grip but it only tightened, until Lee felt the unmistakable snap of the rabbit's neck in his hand. Neither of the boys wanted to take a life but Lee knew to leave the rabbit to suffer in the clutches of the snare would be worse.

Tom prepared the rabbit; taking his hunting knife out he removed the rabbit pelt. Cleaning out the innards, all he was left with was meat ready to be cooked.

Lee watched his brother cautiously prepare the meat, being careful to make sure it was clean and ready for cooking. Tom looked across to Lee, whose eyes were transfixed on his hands and the steps being taken to prepare a meal for them both. Tom spoke in an authoritative way that Lee wasn't really used to.

"Will you get some wood for the fire. I am not preparing the rabbit for decoration. The sooner we get it on, the sooner we can eat!"

Lee knew that the process of killing the rabbit stressed Tom who was not used to seeing something die before him. Neither of them were, but Lee didn't feel the stress over it as Tom did, knowing that it was only by necessity. Lee stood up, wiped the dry dirt from the leg of his pants and casually strolled away to find some dry firewood.

Tom awaited his return so he could add the fresh logs to the fire to make it really roar for cooking the meat and bedding down for the evening. The longer Lee was gone the more he became anxious for his return. Taking his emergency beacon in hand to signal for his father to come, he heard a twig snap off in the distance. Tom went to see if it was his brother who had stood on it, leaving with a degree of urgency and not realising that he left his knife beside the freshly prepared rabbit.

Walking five hundred paces or so, following the track that his brother had left, Tom was able to see where Lee stopped to pick up firewood. He took a moment to silently thank his father for preparing him so well. Tracking was now like a second nature, although the signs were subtle. Lee's tracks stopped abruptly and Tom found a small pile of firewood that Lee had gathered lying on the ground at the base of a tree.

Looking around, but unable to see his brother, Tom heard another twig snap followed by the sound of heavy breathing. Tom spun around, but the chilling figure that greeted him was not that of his brother. Instead his eyes met something he had not anticipated for a second.

Tom's heart dropped in his chest. It took a brief moment for his brain to process the unexpected sight before him. But the large black bear was looking right back at him, challenging him. The bear was fully-grown. Sheer terror gripped Tom as he looked down from the bear's eyes and saw its mouth was dripping with blood. His brain fought with the reality that this could be the blood of his younger brother. Slowly and deliberately he reached for his knife, only to find it wasn't there. He then realised that it was left back with all the equipment. He held his breath and waited to see what the bear would do. Tom knew he was strong enough to kill it, but did not know if his strength made his skin impervious to an attack from a beast such as a bear. If the bear was to make a swipe at him, it could be the end of him.

He bit down his fears and looked the bear directly in the eye, waiting for it to react to his presence. Standing very still the bear looked at him and then reared up on its hind legs in a display of dominance before landing back down on all four legs.

As the bear landed it seemed content that Tom was no threat and turned to walk away. Tom let out a breath of relief and mindlessly shifted his weight from one leg to the other. But before he could do anything about it he heard a snap under his foot, unknowingly having stood on a twig.

The noise disturbed the bear and it turned to face him, but this time there was no show of dominance, there was no warning, the bear began to charge for Tom. There was only one of two things he could do; the first was to play dead; to hit the ground and hope the bear wouldn't see him as a threat. The other option was to hit the bear with all his might before the bear was able to land a blow to him. This was kill or be killed and every nerve in Tom's body was alert to his instincts. His sense of invincibility kicked in and he decided very quickly that if he was going to die that day it would be on his terms, clenching every muscle in his body, standing tall, he braced himself for impact with the bear. The animal covered the ground between himself and Tom in a matter of seconds and as the bear grew closer Tom could see no soul in its eyes, only a beast set on ending his short life.

The bear was about three meters away from him when he heard a loud roar from above his head and the bear's gaze moved up. It was his brother high upon a tree branch, who had flung himself outward from the tree. Flying through the air towards the bear he aimed for its head. As he landed, the animal began growling ferociously. The bear shook his head so Lee would fall, simultaneously trying to grip the boy in his mouth, but Lee held on tightly to the bear's head while trying to free his arm so he could swing his knife at the beast. As the bear let out another growl, he managed to free his arm and plunged his knife into the neck of the bear.

The growl turned into an empty hollow gasp as it tried to recover from the blow. Lee fell off the bear and landed on the ground right in front of him, but the bear had lost interest in the boys and was struggling to stay upright.

It wrangled a bit, stumbling slowly and hitting the forest floor with a pronounced impact. Getting to his feet again, Lee picked his bloodied knife off the ground and went over to the bear, which by now was in a vast amount of pain. Taking his knife and sticking it into the bear's neck once again he freed the animal from the pain it was in. Even though it was the humane thing to do it was not glamorous or glorious. Pushing the knife in, Lee could feel it tearing against muscle, bone and cartilage. Crossing a line that Lee didn't realise he had. His stomach shrank and it pained him to kill what was a beautiful beast. Lee fought his body not to expel the contents of his stomach.

Looking round at his brother, Lee saw Tom frozen, in a state of shock at what he had just witnessed. Seeing something in Lee's eyes he had not seen before; the look of a man possessed.

Moving back to the bear panting heavily, he pulled his knife from the bear's neck, wiped it on his sleeve and turned back to Tom. Lashing out angrily at him he said, "Where is your knife?" But without giving Tom the time to answer he said sternly, "Tom, this isn't a game. You could die here..." pausing to take a breath he began to adjust back to himself, with a tear rolling down his cheek and red in his eyes. "Tom you're my big brother and I need you, I'm not strong like you, I can't take risks like you, but I won't stand by and watch you risk everything..."

Tom saw that the possession in Lee's eyes was in fact fuelled by the fear of losing him and conceded to his younger brother. "You're right, Lee. I'm sorry..."

While the two trekked back to the camp, Lee explained, "I went to gather the firewood and I came across the bear tracks, hearing the twig break in the bush across from me, I scaled the tree and waited for the bear to pass hopefully unseen.

However, when you happened below where I was, I had no choice when the bear attacked but to use the element of surprise. I had to take action."

The two boys returned to where the camp was set, cooked and ate the rabbit and bedded down for the night. They were both in a degree of shock, still having adrenaline pumping from the bear attack and were unable to sleep. Stretched out, looking up at the night sky through the cover of the trees, they struggled to settle. Tom spoke up and broke the relative silence.

"I actually can't believe you jumped from the tree."

Lee began to laugh. "Well, what was I supposed to do?"

Tom was bemused. "I don't know, but I definitely didn't expect you to do that… Ninja style!" Both the boys continued to laugh, naturally falling silent after a moment, Tom reflected. "Lee?"

Lee answered "Yea, Tom?"

Tom lay silent for a few minutes and simply said, "Thanks, Lee."

Lee calmed his mind once again thinking of the feat he had performed and the odds of him getting away unhurt as they both thought hard for those few moments about what he would risk for his brother.

"Anytime bro."

The next day they woke and walked at a steady pace the

rest of the way back to the cabin, where their father seemed surprised to see they made it down so quickly. Inquiring about the hike, they told him everything about their days in the wilderness. About how they didn't bed down on the first night until they got below the snow line and how they found fresh water, and how they snared the rabbit for dinner. Fearing the repercussions of their actions regarding the bear they decided not to tell their father about that as he wouldn't have approved of the risk either of them took.

Philip, being the protective man that he was, didn't leave his sons alone on the mountain, but rather had tracked them from behind, to ensure their safety. Not being able to see the incident with the bear, as he was further back, he came across the bear's body and from the tracks left on the ground he worked out what had happened.

The only thing he didn't know was which of his two sons killed the bear and which of his sons was nearly killed by it. Removing both the large and sharp incisor teeth from the bear's mouth, he placed them in a handkerchief and put it carefully into his bag.

Philip assumed that it would have been Lee that got into trouble, him being younger and more vulnerable to attack, which was the case until he was sorting their gear out after their return. Both of the boys' blades had small traces of blood and animal hair on them so he was unsure, but when taking Lee's shirt and seeing where he had cleaned the blade on his sleeve it became clear that it was Lee who saved the life of his older stronger brother.

Philip did not expect that Lee had strength in him to undergo such a feat and come away both unhurt and stronger for it. He was proud that he knew the boys were looking out for each other and would work as a team to protect each other even from him, but he was also fearful that Lee would risk everything for his brother.

Lee took the knife and wrapped it in a cloth and slipped it into his bag. Once again sniggering to Tom that his gift was something he already owned, but really knowing that it was a lot more.

CHAPTER SIX

The two boys were close their entire life. Tom would often take Lee to sporting events and take him out while playing golf. He liked golf as his strength allowed him to hit the ball further than most, but he struggled with his putting game, as he didn't have the delicate touch needed. This frustrated him at times, but it wasn't so much about the game to Tom as it was about spending time with his brother. They got along as strong friends and although the typical sibling relationship was never far from erupting into an old-school style scuffle, their underlying respect for each other kept these scuffles friendly and as they grew up their friendship only became stronger.

One Saturday the boys were playing a morning round and midway around the course Lee was struggling to carry Tom's bag, so he took it from Lee and led the way over to a big tree in the middle of the fairway. Tom sat down under the tree, unzipping the pouch on the side of the bag. He reached his hand in and pulled out a brown bag of fries that he had bought the night before. Tom opened the bag, reached inside, pulled a hand full of fries for himself and offered the rest of the bag to Lee. "Here Lee, have a couple of these!"

Lee reached his hand out, taking the bag from his brother. Lee pulled a handful out for himself and ate the first few, even though they were cold and didn't taste very appealing. Happily, Lee ate away, never complaining as they were something shared with his brother, something special for the two to share with no one around as the world would pass by. And this was how it always was between them. Somehow, losing their mother at such young ages had created an unbreakable bond between them, leaving them happy in one another's company, against the world together.

After a while other golfers would play while the two boys sat watching them try to perfect their swings. Tom watched the technique of the different players in order to further his own game. Lee watched more bewildered than anything with the style of clothes and all the audacious colours. Palette combinations that he would have never seen before brought an expression of amusement to his face.

"I think that would look good on you," Tom said, observing his brother.

Lee looked back befuddled, "I don't think so."

Tom packed away what remained of the fries into the golf bag, pulling out a bottle of flat cola offering some to Lee. Each quenched their thirst and continued to finish the round of golf.

This memory lived with Lee, comforting him for the rest of his days, secure in the knowledge that his big brother was there for him and would remain there. The time they spent together was precious, each knowing the lifelong cost of losing those important to you, making them respect each other and their father in a way that most teenagers wouldn't learn until later life.

By the time Lee turned sixteen he was attending school like any normal kid his age and was on track to becoming a great man. The principles that his father had taken great time and effort to instil in him were evident in the way he treated his friends and teachers. To all around he seemed to be a hard working boy, with an understanding of the world that you would expect from a much older man. But when it came down to it, he was still a teenager, trying to find his place in the world and struggling without the presence of his loving mother. Over time he developed a major passion for music, finding that the sentiment of songwriting often mirrored his own feelings. He listened to the bands of the day and was partial to the older music that his father was interested in, finding it easy to relax and shut off from his constant inner monologue about his shortcomings from not having an ability. Philip would often watch as Lee sat staring into space with headphones on, oblivious to the world around him but with a look on his face that spoke volumes. He worried for his son, so much more introverted than Tom.

Together the boys played on the football team in his school and like most sixteen-year-old boys, they had an eye for the ladies. The two boys passed their weekends watching sports and movies. They spent hours debating over them, arguing about team tactics and the plot line in their preferred films.

Whilst always shying away from the topic of his powers, in

general this was seen as a personal one, like a person's sexuality or age. No one really discussed it as for every power that a person had there was also a corresponding weakness; as unique to the individual as the ability itself.

Most people didn't know about their own weakness unless they were exposed to it and in general if they were exposed to it they would not live to talk about it, unless intervention from an outside source came to help. Sometimes within the bravado of the schoolyard people challenged each other. On these occasions his brother helping him conceal the fact that Lee lacked any hidden ability.

He took joy in setting up elaborate feats, where Tom would use his strength and make it look like Lee was doing it. It would be something as simple as Tom lifting a small car off the ground then challenging any of his classmates to an arm wrestle, beating them easily then challenging his brother and always letting Lee win after what seemed a titanic struggle between the two. This was a regular sight in the schoolyard.

On other occasions the pair would appear to fight over things that were irrelevant. Sometimes Lee would win, sometimes Tom, forgetting to let Lee win. They were a team and they protected each other and most importantly they protected Lee's secret. Seeing Lee's feats of strength, no other student would dare challenge him and on the rare occasion that they did, either Tom would have Lee's back or Lee depended on his heightened awareness and intellect to get him through whatever obstacle was thrown in his path. As a team they worked very well together, but when Tom went off to college things were a little harder for Lee.

Without his brother around Lee no longer had someone to keep an eye on him, to watch over his actions from a distance and, if need be, to come to his aid. But Lee proved himself as capable and self-reliant as he had when he came to his brothers' aid from the bear. Lee had never taken Tom's efforts to conceal his lack of ability for granted. It was above and beyond the call of duty, and without these little tricks Lee would have been left exposed to the reality of the world that he just didn't quite fit into. He was strong willed and determined to be able to protect his own secret without the help of any other person, so he actively resolved to spend the rest of his school life going unnoticed.

Never meeting his potential as a student or as an athlete, Lee remained under the radar for the rest of his school life. In a world with no powers, Lee would have excelled, with his keen intellect and observational skills, but in this world he had no choice but to keep to himself, maintaining the relationship with his family and choosing not to connect with others for fear of being exposed. Other kids involved in sports weren't allowed to use their power as it was seen as an unfair advantage and it also taught kids that relying on your capabilities wasn't advisable to get ahead in life. Given this restriction on sporting prowess Lee had a natural advantage as his father raised him as an athlete. But he never used this advantage, never finishing last in a race and never finishing first. Lee went unseen throughout the rest of his schooling life.

Without his brother in the school to support him he reverted inwardly with the burden of the secret he had to carry. He felt like he was lying to both himself and the world, as if he was being untrue to his character and his inner self, holding back and being false to the world.

It seemed to weigh on him, a fact that was not lost on Philip who always kept a watchful eye over his son. He grasped that this was a burden his son would have to carry for all his days and that it was something he would have to learn to deal with himself. For this reason, he was reluctant to intervene and hoped that his son would be strong enough to face the challenges that lay ahead of him. Despite the heavy weight of this burden, Philip saw his son growing into a man with strong principles and an objective view of the world around him, his heart filling with pride for the son he had dedicated his life to raising. He knew that his wife would be proud of the man Lee was growing up to be, regardless of whether he had a power or not.

Every so often Lee found the tediousness of school getting to him. He struggled with hiding his intellect and often found himself bored in class learning things that were unchallenging to him. He'd find himself sitting there, looking around at his classmates who he neither knew well nor cared about, refusing to get caught up in their childish games and bullying. He would always finish the work set for them in record time, leaving him with nothing to do but wait for the others, while he became lost in his head, dreaming of a time when he was his own man and could do what he wanted with his time.

When the tediousness and boredom became too much to handle he would skip class. Leaving for school like normal in the morning, then waiting for his father to leave for work, Lee would sneak back into the house and spend the day on the couch watching old films. He knew that if he was caught out, the disappointment in his father's eyes would cut right through him, but sometimes the thought of walking into that school, totally invisible to those around him, was just too much to bear. Whereas, the comfort of his own home and the pull of a lazy day on the sofa felt like a more constructive use of his time.

The days of skipping school became a bad habit that crept into Lee's week. On one such day after exhausting his collection of movies and resigning himself to channel-hoping, he sat mindlessly flicking through the stations looking at what passed as entertainment. Boredom had set in.

Not wanting to watch another show in which people aired their dirty laundry for all to see, he turned off the television and glanced around the room for something to keep himself entertained with. His eye was drawn to his father's old mahogany writing desk that sat in the corner of the room, propped up against the wall as one of its legs was missing.

Looking at the desk he knew that this was where his father kept all his old music books. Recalling a song about a jail in Birmingham that his father used to sing to him and his brother on road trips up to the cabin, Lee thought he would like to learn it.

He wandered over to the bench, sat himself in front of the desk and started to look through the songbooks. After searching for a while and finding the song he wanted, he sat there trying to memorise the lyrics.

Growing bored of the monotony of learning just one set of lyrics, he scanned his eye across the desk. Seeing an old photo album at the bottom of a pile of books, sliding the album out, he took it in his hands and began to examine it. While looking at it, it was obvious it hadn't been opened in a long time, as there was a fine layer of dust. Blowing off the top layer, any residual dust that was left he wiped away with his fingers. Upon opening the album, the spine cracked as if to verify that it hadn't been looked at in an age. He peeled back each page and was greeted with pictures of his father when he was young, accompanied by his mother.

This was the first time he'd seen his parents as a young couple, it was strange for him to see this and he found comfort in the picture they presented. While peering at the pictures the obvious joy they had came shining through. But as much as the happy scenes spread before him warmed his heart, he was struggling with a degree of conflict. If it was not for him she would still be here and his father wouldn't have faced such toil.

But Lee appreciated that wishing his own existence away was not going to help anyone, but rather cause him inner turmoil, so he tried to stay away from such thoughts.

Sitting and flicking through the album a little while more, beholding his father's memories, he felt a sense of loss for something he had never had. Turning over the last page there was no picture, just an old delicate sheet of paper that was frayed around the edges and folded in half. Slipping out the sheet of paper he left the album open on the desk.

Unfolding the sheet, he saw the familiar handwriting of his father. It was a note he had written to his mother a few years after her death, the date in the corner of the sheet said that it was eleven years old. Lee began to read the words his father wrote for his mother, knowing she would never hear them;

Sit
Come and see me
Down by the waterfront
Where the hills roll into the sea
Meet me along the path where the old harbour
Used to be

Realise it's me
Bring your eyes to meet mine
Look fondly towards me

Walk awhile

Tell me how your dreams have come to be

Sit by my side and we can
Watch the sun disappear
Let the night and infinite stars' creep near

The light in the lighthouse has long
gone out

If you'll be my North Star,
I'll be your South.

Sitting for a while absorbing what he had just read, he thought over his relationship with his father and the contrast of the relationship between his parents, the loss his father had suffered and how he managed to conceal his hurt from his sons. Conflict hit Lee again, for had he not existed his mother would still be here and he wondered, would his family be happier in a world where she lived on and he didn't? Lee sat in perfect silence, unaware of the fact that his father had returned to the house and was standing in the room, behind him.

The silence broke with Philip asking, "Why aren't you in school?" this startled Lee, who was still holding the note in his hand.

He dropped his hand to his side and stammered, "I… I wasn't feeling too good, so I came home."

Philip was less interested in his response as he was in the reason his son was sitting at his writing desk. Approaching to see what he was doing, he looked down over his shoulder and saw the photo album open on the desk.

Letting out a soft breath as if to hide a chuckle, Philip ran his hand up his neck and scratched his rough chin as he spoke to Lee, "I remember that day well..." Pausing in contemplation he lifted the album up and uttered, "I haven't looked at this in what seems a lifetime."

Sitting on the bench beside his son he flicked through the pages of memories. Getting to the end he closed the album and sat it back on the desk. Looking toward his son he noticed his eyes focused down to something by his side in his hand. He asked quizzically, "What have you got there?"

Lee, uncertain of himself and not knowing if he had done something wrong turned to his father. Nervously, he raised his hand with the poem in it and handed it to him.

Philip took the piece of paper in one hand and used the other to prop up his chin as if to ponder and commenced reading his own words. Reading the first few lines it became clear to him what he was actually reading. It was the memory of an emotion he had experienced a lifetime ago. After finishing reading the words he folded the page and placed it on the table in front of him.

They both sat in silence for a minute or two, or what seemed to be that long. Philip placed his hand reassuringly on his son's leg and began to talk.

"I know you have been struggling lately. I know it's not fair on you to be carrying the burden of what you have had to conceal about yourself while still trying to fit in, but I have been doing the best I can for you. I am not as equipped to deal with matters of delicacy as your mother was, if she was sitting here she would know exactly what to say to you.

You know she bought me this old desk, when we got it the leg was already broken off; it was the best worst present I have ever received, if that makes sense. When I look at you, I see her. I see her every time and it kills me to know you are struggling. I know that I can't help you as I should. I tried to prepare you to deal with anything the world can throw at you physically and mentally, but maybe I lacked showing you how to deal emotionally. I find it hard to show those things. Your mother could just look at me and she would know exactly how I felt. She would draw out my emotions as well as her own..."

Philip paused for a second to clear his throat and wiped away some tears that had begun to gather in his eyes. Lee kept his face turned downward so as to not make his father self-conscious of the situation. Instead just listening as his father spoke on.

"The day you were born my whole life got thrown on its head. Joey and I had plans, but they were ruled out that day. When she left, she gave me one final gift. That was you, son. With her last breath she gave you your name..."

Lee raised his head slightly on hearing this. He had never been told this story before and continued to listen to his father.

"Sorry for asking you to carry this burden alone, but it's something you must do, for your own safety and protection. I might have been wrong in the way I raised you, but I feel now as I did then, that it's the best thing for you. When your mother passed I became drained of all outward emotion, it doesn't mean I don't feel everything inside, because I do. I am just not strong enough to show it. I love you son, I don't say that enough, but I do and one day you will find someone who will make you feel as your mother made me feel.

Even when that happens I want you to be very careful who you trust with your secret. Relationships end and there is a thin line between love and hate. If your secret gets out, you will be in inherent danger and if that happens you will need an exit strategy. I am proud of you son, so be careful and be kind to yourself. I can already see the kind of man you are becoming and I am nothing but proud..."

He reached out to the desk, opened a drawer and took a handkerchief out, wiping his eyes, cleared his nose and stood up to walk away. Halfway across the room he turned one more time to face his son. "And, Lee..." Lee didn't respond. He just turned his head towards where his father was standing and waited for him to continue, "...Don't skip school again." He didn't answer, but nodded in acknowledgment.

As his father left, he just sat there and reflected on what had just happened. Sitting in silence he once again flicked through the photo album in front of him, not so much looking at the pictures this time, but rather just to have something to focus on. To every young person their father is the strongest person in the world and this is this first time that Lee saw his father not as a man with superhuman strength, but as a man; a normal man who had to face the trials and tribulations of everyday life and far from being infallible he was actually quite flawed.

Lee took strength from this. He didn't need a shrouded ability to be a man. The definition of what made him good and complete was not what was reflected out; rather what was reflected in. Knowing the measure of a man was being able to face the world head on and not hide away or complain when it knocks you on your ass. From then on Lee would face anything the world could throw at him head on and not hide away, all the while keeping his secret.

CHAPTER SEVEN

When Lee finished high school he achieved an average grade and subsequently attended an average college where he got an average degree. But this average life was all he strove for, knowing that any undue attention would cause problems, but continuing to stay under the radar for what would probably be his entire life was exhausting. Lee needed a challenge. He wanted to really work for something that he could look at with pride. He wanted Tom and his father to be proud of him and not just because they loved him. Not just because they had to. He carried around a constant feeling of dissatisfaction that niggled at him, no matter what he did and it was only getting worse.

After leaving college Lee began working in the Post Newspaper as a junior editor on the news desk, allowing him to feed his appetite for information. His main role was to read through stories submitted by journalists and make sure they were both accurate and correct. With this Lee was able to expand his already impressive mind learning stories of heroism and villainous misdoings. The inspiration he found in these stories only served to increase his belief that there must be more to his life; there needed to be more than just flying under the radar of the powers that be.

Although there was peace for the most part, there was still an undercurrent of crime that wasn't really seen in everyday life, the fact of which Lee knew all too well from his encounter with Jimmy. This tide of crime mostly came from underground clubs where men tested their might against each other for venture and position within the resurgence of an elite spate of crime bosses, who emerged when the borders were opened up between the two governments.

They viewed the United New World as an untapped territory where they could make a lot of money through illegal activity, whilst remaining loyal to the Old World Alliance. Newspapers didn't tend to print stories relating to any negative societal activities, but given Lee's position within the paper he was privy to the stories before they were inevitably pulled. He also had the opportunity to learn about business, economics and investments.

On lonely nights he learned how to trade the markets and was very successful at it. Finally, he had found a challenge that he could excel at without drawing attention to himself. He could see the whole market and account for variables and political factors. It nearly became like a game to him, like one his father would have given him years before. He learned to read the information before him and make logical decisions on the outcome of market investment. He set up ghost companies so that the money trail couldn't be linked back to him and by doing so he gave himself a cushion of security that would help keep him financially secure for the rest of his life, making sure he could keep up his job as it helped feed his thirst for knowledge and helped him to be seen as a normal guy.

Tom's life in contrast was rather different. Given the strength, training and discipline his father instilled on him, he went to join the army. Even though there were no wars of significance, each country maintained an army as a deterrent. As hidden capabilities weren't openly talked about within the remit of a person's application to become a soldier, many soldiers masked their abilities, opting rather to gain promotion through the traditional routes. This also protected the soldier from being utilised as an ability, rather than a person. Tom was one of these soldiers, but given his upbringing and his awareness for the world around him he quickly proved himself to be a valuable asset to the army as a reconnaissance soldier.

Tom even got awarded the medal of valour for his outstanding acts of bravery. On a mission in the forest, Tom was to recon a village where suspected terrorists had kidnapped a bus full of school girls. His mission was simple; get in, identify the presence of the schoolgirls and radio for back up. The village had only one road in or out with a well-built wooden bridge over the village stream making it difficult for unseen entry. With nightfall's cover Tom waded his way up the stream using the water to cover his scent from the guard dogs until he got to the bridge, where two guards stood with their ever-ready dogs.

In complete silence and darkness Tom rigged the bridge with explosives making pursuit of escaping prisoners and soldiers impossible. The expected time on the mission was ten minutes so Tom set the timer for 15, allowing five minutes to locate the kids and radio back up.

Having placed the final explosive, Tom waded further up stream, found cover and pulled himself out of the stream and began to search the village. Working his way through all the buildings, he hid in shadows, hunting for any signs of the girls or bus. Finding his way round the village Tom discovered a barn hidden to the rear of what appeared to him to be the village church.

Peering in the window, Tom came across the bus the girls were taken from hidden under a tarp. Snatching the radio from his bag, he turned on the radio to break silence and call it in. First Class Sergeant McKay, who was Tom's sergeant and had come through the academy with him, was to lead the extraction team once Tom confirmed the presence of the hostages. Tom radioed in that he had discovered the bus and continued to search. As he moved to the next building to his horror he spied the extraction team moving in too early, way too early. Tom got back in the radio calling in his mission abort code but he was too late. The extraction team had breached the village. Tom knew the only possibility now to save the hostages was to hope that while the terrorists were busy with the extraction team he could move freely from building to building.

Dashing over and back across the village, he scanned every building as he darted by, trying to locate the captives. One building caught Tom's attention. The guards on the door did not budge despite all hell breaking loose around them. Flanking from the side, Tom pulled out his gun and shot one in the foot. He collapsed to the ground, crying out as the other guard made ready his weapon, but it was too late. Leaping through the air with full force, Tom struck his knee squarely in the guard's chest. Landing on top of his crumpled body Tom placed the gun to his head, gripped the trigger and released a round. Tom spun around and fired once more at the other guard still clenching his foot.

Gun cocked, Tom hit the door shoulder first, busting

open all locks and most of the door frame as he entered the
building.

Nothing, there was nothing in the room. No girls,
nothing. Stunned, Tom turned to make his escape when he heard
a rustle from inside the building. Spinning around and pointing
his gun into the obviously empty room, Tom knew he wasn't
alone. Searching and finding nothing except a sporadic sound of
whimpering, he put down his gun and spoke out.

"I am here to get you out," still nothing was revealed.
Speaking softly. "Trust me!"

From behind a projected masking, one child stepped out,
then another and another. Tom found himself in a room of
scared girls and constructed a plan in his head to get them out
while shielding them from the battle outside. "Put the masking
back up, conceal us all." A child stepped forward and threw the
masking cloak up in the air, covering all the girls along with Tom.
He moved to the back of the room and throwing his fist straight
at the wall on the poorly constructed building, he blew a hole in

it large enough for a child to slip through.

Approaching the opening, a small child went to pass through. Taking her hand, Tom bent down on his knees and calmly said, "No, we are going out the front door, and straight over the bridge." Turning to the child with masking capabilities, Tom asked, "What's your name?"

Nervous and unsure, the child responded, "Annie…"

"Such a brave girl, keeping all your friends safe, now I need you to try to keep them safe a little longer. While I get you out. Can you do this?"

Annie looked away from Tom, scared by his appearance but comforted by his words and simply stated, "Yes."

"Can anything come into the mask you don't allow in?" queried Tom.

"NO, nothing," Annie responded.

Tom realised he could keep them safe. "Great. Let's go!"

He opened the door and, masked by Annie, guided the girls out. Moving across the dirt road that ran up the middle of the village Tom brought the girls to the bridge. Here he was met by a single solitary enemy combatant. Blocking the escape route Tom crouched on his knee, turning to Annie. "Wait until he moves and we will simply walk out of here."

Annie for the first time looked Tom in the eye and said, "He can see you!"

Hearing this Tom shot his attention back to the soldier on the bridge, but it was too late; a searing pain hit his shoulder.

Falling under the weight of his body and the pain inflicted, Tom could feel metal grinding against his bone. Not wincing or shouting out, Tom simply got angered by the pain that coursed through him. He quickly deduced that this soldier's ability was to do with his sight. Being able to see through the masked veil that covered him and the kids meant he must have had heat vision or something similar. Not taking any time to actually figure out exactly what his ability was, Tom attacked.

Tom, stealth-like and fast, ran straight at the soldier who emptied his weapons clip back at him in a futile attempt to stop his advance. Tom danced around the bullets as they whizzed past his head, gaining momentum as a bullet hit his thigh but it did not slow him. Reaching the man, Tom leapt once more, fist at the ready and threw it into the man's skull as his head snapped back with a deep grinding crunch. Falling to the ground dead, Tom stood over him, grimacing and pissed off that he just been shot… again.

Guiding the girls to the extraction point, Tom awaited the return of the team. Checking his watch and seeing there were only two minutes until the charges were due to go off, he knew something was wrong. Wanting to go and help, he knew he couldn't leave the girls. They were too vulnerable, most being too young to use their powers and Annie's power had begun to wain from exhaustion. He knew he couldn't leave. So he waited, and in waiting he could hear the charges he set explode and illuminate the sky from quite a distance away.

Waiting for any signs of his comrade's return and guarding the girls, he radioed for the chopper to come, as it did not look good. The chopper came quickly and Tom helped the kids on board. As he helped the last on, Tom turned and ran away from the chopper back in the direction of the village. The chopper waited for him but he did not return alone, emerging from the tree line with someone sprawled over his shoulder. Tom ran towards the chopper that now hovered above the ground in anticipation of his immediate entry. Tom threw the body of the man into the chopper and jumped in. Holding the man at his feet safe, he let out a breath of relief. The co-pilot of the chopper rolled his head round and asked shockingly, "Is that it?"

Tom was struck with sadness and couldn't reply but nodded his head in confirmation.

"Who is it? I need to radio it in!"

"It's Sergeant McKay," Tom replied as he sat back in his seat and looked out from the chopper at the devastation left behind.

The subsequent military inquest into what happened that night found McKay to be at fault for leading his men into the village before Tom called it in, despite his protests that Tom should have been found at fault for the disaster. Tom's actions won him the medal of valour; McKay's actions cost him the lives of 14 soldiers and nearly ended his career. He was transferred to another division and Tom was promoted.

*

Lee shied away from the fact that his brother had an elevated profile, not wanting to add to his own, but the two brothers remained close into adulthood even though they didn't see each other as often, as Tom travelled a lot with his job. Each time they saw each other, whether it had been just the night before, a month before or 6 months, it was as if they had never been separated. Conversation ran smoothly, jokes bubbled between them and they both felt secure in the knowledge that they had each other's backs, both physically, mentally and emotionally. Philip had brought them up to value family above all else and this came as naturally to them as the abilities that they did or didn't have.

Lee grew comfortable within his routine, working in the paper for a few years and also playing the markets in secret, growing his nest egg. By his twenty-eighth birthday, through hard work and persistence, he became a senior editor at the paper and had enough money to last him two lifetimes, although he continued to maintain a modest lifestyle, finding it not only allowed him to live unnoticed, but was also a lifestyle he enjoyed, given his upbringing.

Despite his financial and professional success, Lee couldn't escape a lost feeling in himself. The persona reflected outwardly was that of a relatively successful man, but inwardly at times he felt empty. Unfulfilled by TV dinners and midnight stock market trading, he began to feel burdened once again with the secret he carried. Removed from the human touch he craved so much but had to avoid, he kept people at arm's length. He often found himself longing for more and began to think that the longing that yearned inside him would be cured when he found another person to share part of his life with. Lee was very careful not to let anyone know of this feeling. It was less that he was looking for love but rather that he craved companionship; someone with whom he wouldn't feel like so much of an outsider, someone he didn't have to hide from. Lee was in effect seeking his counterpoint.

CHAPTER EIGHT

On a day like any other, he stopped to get a coffee in in the same shop that was his refuge when he needed. Normally he would get it to go, unless evading the police, but as it was raining on this day, and having ignored the advice given to him earlier by the weatherman to take an umbrella, he opted to sit awhile and drink in the neighbourhood until the rain lifted.

The rain seemed to persist as if to keep him from leaving and by now any remnants of the heat that had been in the end of his coffee had long dispelled and the foam that was Lees favourite part of a coffee was now crystallised with the sugar, coating the base of the coffee cup. Lee put the cup to the side and stopped thinking back about the past, letting a deep breath out as he relaxed his shoulders back and released the growing tension in his neck. Instead he turned his attention elsewhere, trying to enjoy what remained of his day off.

Sitting by the window he watched the world pass for a while and found himself daydreaming. He watched the people, some on their own and some with friends, lovers and families. His family was strong, supportive and always there for him, but it wasn't enough. He wondered if this was a selfish thought, as he had a family that so many people could only dream of. Not only were they supportive and loving, but he was also fantastic friends with both his brother and father, and never got bored or frustrated with their company. What he was frustrated with was that this was it. There was no one to hold hands with as he walked through the rain. No one to hold an umbrella over protectively. His parents had been lucky enough to have true romance and while it had been snatched away from them far too early, they still had it. For those few years they were everything to each other, and together they created two new lives and a whole world for their little family. Could Lee ever hope for such a thing? Could he ever be accepted for the person that he was, deep down, and let someone love him, powerless as he was?

Watching the rain bounce off the window he noticed how

people were seemingly dancing through the rain in desperation not to get wet. The futility of this endeavour made Lee smile quietly to himself. Whilst lost in his thoughts, he failed to notice the girl sitting across smiling at him from behind her book. As he continued to daydream the girl began to laugh at him. Her laugh was so endearing it brought Lee's eyes to meet hers, playing with an old dull locket that sat around her neck as the warmth of her smile emanated out. Slightly startled and embarrassed, he adjusted his demeanour. The girl continued to smile at him and after a moment she said, "Are you enjoying yourself?"

Lee responded to the girl with a warm inviting half smile, "Yea, I kind of am I suppose..."

Standing up and walking towards him, it was only now that Lee was able to take in what he was faced with. He couldn't take his eyes from her beautiful big eyes and warm smile, as she sat down by him.

"Hi I'm Jennifer, Jennifer Patzner..."

Conversation flowed naturally and he learned that she actually worked in the coffee shop and was on a break.

He queried about the book she was reading and she paused, looking him straight in the eye and smiling. It was so refreshing for a guy to actually take an interest. She wasn't oblivious to her looks and was quietly confident of her feminine features, but recently she had come to feel completely fed up of guys only being interested in flirting as she shied away from human contact. But she had too. As soon as she spoke of something close to her heart or made a remotely intelligent comment she could see the light fade from their eyes. Yet here was this man, holding her eye contact and seemingly completely interested in what she had to say. She dove straight in to telling him all about it.

"The Picture of Dorian Gray. It is one of my all-time favourite books." Lifting the book in her hand she flicked through the pages of the battered old copy and continued to tell him about the story. "It's about a young man who sold his soul for eternal youth. His secret had cost him so much in his life, all for the pursuit of an eternal state of ecstasy."

Lee saw similarities with the secret Dorian Gray had to keep and the secret he kept himself, although he felt no such ecstasy. Lee's upbringing made him into an analytical and logical man. The only art form he really enjoyed was music and he found Jennifer's openness and knowledge of all art forms endearing as she spoke with pure passion from the heart. Her eyes sparkled, as she got lost in what she was saying. Never had he met a woman so captivating.

He didn't want to seem like the empty shell of a person that he felt like, so he focused on things that brought passion into his life. He told her about how close he was to his family and how both his brother and his father were real inspirations in guiding him to become the man that he was. He explained the main piece of wisdom that his father tried to instil in him and how it was a very basic piece of information that his father would repeat to him countless times, with the words, "Trust your gut, it won't lie to you, if something doesn't feel right it's wrong." Lee went on to talk about how his father opened his mind up to music and how listening to music together was how they spent countless nights when Lee was growing up.

The conversation went on for another forty minutes. It flowed easily between them, each one picking up where the other left off, inspired by their words and looking deep into their own lives to find points of similarity. Without even noticing they were building up a network of common ground, becoming more and more trusting with each tale they told. They both exchanged stories of growing up, their careers and everything in between.

Jennifer paused for a moment, toying with the cup in her hands before looking up at Lee with big eyes. He could tell she was contemplating saying something, but he kept quiet for fear of unintentionally putting her off. Instead he simply held her gaze and tried to encourage her with his warmest smile. She bit her lip and looked down at her cup once more. Then, taking a breath in, she playfully teased Lee about the fact that she had seen him come in and out of the coffee shop on a few occasions, but always seeming in a hurry, too much of a hurry for him to see her and to notice the fact that she was quietly trying to catch his eye. She looked down the whole time she spoke, only looking up to see his response as she finished speaking. She looked heartbreakingly beautiful at that moment, with her mix of insecurity and playful eagerness.

"How could I have missed that?"

Jennifer shyly looked down at her hands, "Well I guess you just weren't looking."

She then paused for a moment, taking a sip of the drink she had been using to warm her hands. "But to be fair this is the first time I've actually seen you sit in with your drink. You are normally in and out of here. Suppose I can thank the rain for making you take a moment to yourself."

Through a burgeoning smile Lee gleefully proclaimed, "I'm glad it rained today."

The smile she gave in return was instant, and Lee could see the tension visibly release from her shoulders. He knew that whatever was between them was mutual.

After a while Jennifer was telling Lee a story about when

she was young and trying to fit in at school, and she dropped her book. At that moment both she and Lee reached to pick it up. His hand seemed to reach out and meet hers half way to picking up the book. Lee gave a little chuckle as if to say how absurd the scenario was.

Looking at her he declared, "There is no way we are that cheesy." and smiled warmly.

Jennifer's expression on the other hand was a mixture of confusion and intrigue; she nervously pushed her hand alongside her head and back down to the top of her neck. Gazing up at Lee she said, "I know this might seem odd, but would you hold my hand for a minute."

Lee, taken aback by how forward this girl he had just met was, answered, "Eh… Yea… Sure." and placing his hand in hers, Lee became lost in her eyes; not being able to look anywhere else even though Jennifer's eyes firmly fixated in the direction of their intertwined hands.

After a few seconds Lee took a deep breath, drawing her attention back to him, staring him in the eyes.

"I don't know what it is, but there is something very different about you..."

Lee laughed nervously and replied, "I hope that's a good thing..."

"It's more than good..."

He suddenly contemplated that what she was saying might have something to do with his power or lack thereof, so reluctantly withdrew his hand from hers. He didn't know what her power was, and while he knew many people's, there was no telling whether she had a power that he had ever experienced before. A touch of dread seeped into his chest as he contemplated this, the very thought of it contradicting how he felt about her so far.

Jennifer, once again playing with her locket, watched Lee as his facial expression betrayed the range of emotions he went through in a matter of mere seconds. She could tell that there was something hidden inside of Lee; a secret that he would not be sharing with her anytime soon. She wondered whether it was simply a past gone bad, affecting his present and future, or if it was something more sinister, perhaps something relating to his power, whatever that might be. She composed her face, giving a gentle smile with her eyes. The last thing that she wanted was for this sweet, intelligent man to withdraw from her, after they had spent the last hour getting to know each other at record speed. So she completely changed the topic, circling back to aspirations of what they wanted to do with their lives, what inspired them and just about every other topic under the sun. She had a feeling that the two of them would never run out of things to talk about.

Seeing her once again rub the locket on her chain and the obvious emotional attachment she had with it, Lee enquired, "That's a lovely locket, have you had it long?"

"Yes, I've had it since I was little; my dad gave it to my mother." Her demeanour and tone saddened "When he died, my mother gave it to me to help comfort me. I have worn it every day since; I literally never took it off after she put it on." Opening the locket, peering at the old reproductions of her parents inside, keeping it close she hid the pictures from Lee's line of sight as, having only just met him, sharing this part of her life wasn't easy, and brought no comfort.

Seeing her discomfort and relating to her pain, Lee proclaimed, "I am so sorry, losing a parent is hard. I never knew my mother." Sharing this small piece of himself both reassured and consoled her.

The conversation ended as Jennifer was called back to work, but they exchanged numbers before parting. As she was sauntering away she peered back and through a half smile and with bright eyes she said coyly, "Now don't lose that number. I don't give it to every boy I meet..."

With that Lee reassured her, "Trust me, I won't..." and left the shop. Lee struggled with the concept of holding back his intentions towards Jennifer. He was both excited and scared at the prospect of meeting a girl like her, somehow sensing a safeness with her, someone who didn't push for answers to questions Lee could not feel comfortable with.

He called her within the hour of getting her number, but was worried that his angst would be viewed as a negative in her eyes. He had shied away from true affection and intimacy for the previous years of his life, scared of letting anyone too close for fear they would learn his secret. He put aside his nervousness and picked up the phone, after entering her number wrong three times due to nervousness he began to wonder if she gave him a wrong number. But he knew that this was unlikely and that the person she was wouldn't be inclined to do something like this. He was also certain that she wasn't an Italian restaurant as that was who he had called three times.

He attempted to dial a fourth time. Slowly entering each digit and then double-checking to see if it was right. After checking the last digit, he hit the dial button and tentatively waited. The phone rang a couple of times and then it answered. A soft voice said "Hello." Lee could tell her voice already and it seemed familiar.

"Hi Jennifer. Its Lee from the coffee…" She interrupted him happily before he could finish.

"Hi Lee, how are you?"

It was with this conversation that Lee was finally able to be connected to another person outside his small family. The sound of Jennifer's voice, the easy conversation, everything about her made him relax and feel, for once in his life, that he wasn't missing out on something that everyone else had.

Jennifer found Lee's vulnerable yet paradoxically confident nature intriguing and the strength of feeling that Lee felt was mirrored in her. With nothing holding them back, the two began to date each other. This was to be the start of the first proper relationship Lee was to have since leaving college, so some of the waters ventured remained uncharted to him. They began to see each other regularly and quickly grew comfortable in each other's company. The relationship may have started off slowly as he would always shy away from certain topics in order to conceal any clues as to his abilities and lack thereof, but the strength of feeling between them developed at an alarming speed.

Lee could never quite dismiss the feeling that Jennifer would eventually have to know about his powerlessness, but he felt so at ease in her company that he frequently pushed the thought away from the front of his mind, preferring to be in the present moment with her. Jennifer on the other hand was excited to be with Lee and seemed to want to accelerate the relationship whenever she could.

Finally, she had found her match; someone who stimulated her physically, mentally and emotionally and she was not shy about showing how much she wanted him in her life. Lee couldn't help but notice her attempts to move things forward; simple little things like wanting to meet his family early in the relationship and talking about their future together. Whenever he became aware of this happening he tended to slow things down.

He would often say to her, "It's not about the speed in which it takes us to get to the destination; it's about the journey..." When Jennifer heard this she knew that his intentions were true and she just needed to be patient with him.

Often she would find herself saying, "I have the feeling you're holding something back and I'm n o t sure what it is or why." But both of them understood that a relationship was about compromise, finding a balance and a comfort zone in which both of them were happy. But while Lee could see in Jennifer's eyes that she was completely open to him, laying all her trust in him, he was well aware that she probably could not see the same in him. They both knew that he was holding something back and while his feelings for her were strong and pure, how was she to know that the one thing he kept from her was not related to them as a couple.

As he never disclosed his underlying ability to Jennifer she never disclosed hers to him. At times she would playfully tease him that he wouldn't tell her, saying, "I know everything there is to know except this one thing." But it was often delivered with a laugh as she could see Lee would grow visibly uncomfortable. But she also seemed shy of the topic, referring to mistakes in her past when her shrouded ability got the better of her, but never revealing what exactly it was.

Lee knew that he would only have to push her slightly to find out what her power was, as she was always so willing to open up to him and move their relationship forward by sharing everything. However, he would never ask her, because he was not yet ready to share his secret with her yet. With them both keeping their own secrets, somehow it kept them on an even footing; something that Lee felt much more comfortable with at the moment.

CHAPTER NINE

Lee's relationship with Jennifer grew closer and he fondly considered her to be his best friend, naturally sharing a part of himself with her that he simply didn't share with his brother. When Jennifer began to have difficulty with renewing the lease on her apartment, rather than her searching for a new place to live Lee decided it was about time he showed he was willing to commit to her. Trying to think outside the box, he came up with a way to ask her to move in that she wouldn't expect.

"Hey, you need some help looking for a new place? There are plenty of other flats you could rent instead of this one. It's more hassle than it is worth." Lee said as he walked up behind her while she washed the dishes, encircling her with his arms and pulling her body close to his. He nuzzled into her, breathing in the intoxicating smell of freshly washed hair.

Her hands paused in the sink as she considered what he was saying. She was desperate for him to ask her to move in, but the decision needed to be his and she didn't want to pressure him into it. From the sounds of things, her moving in wasn't exactly at the forefront of Lee's mind.

"Erm, yeah that's not a bad idea actually. Some place new might be quite refreshing. I'm sick of this area anyway." In her head she thought about how much she longed to be in Lee's neighbourhood; quiet and slightly rural yet close enough to the city to be suitable for her job. It would just be perfect, in every way. Waking up next to him every single morning was all she wanted.

"Well I walked past an estate agent the other day actually."

Jennifer's eyebrows shot up at this unexpected comment.

"And I went in to ask about a few places. I could take you now for some viewings if you wanted?" He leant his back against the kitchen counter opposite the sink, allowing her room to react and turn around.

"What? Oh. Yeah that would be good. Right now?"

Seeing Jennifer so unsure and yet still open to the situation warmed Lee's heart. *This is going to make her day,* he thought.

"Yeah, why not! We can make a day of it."

She did not look convinced, but always happy to humour Lee, she agreed and went to grab her coat and bag.

Lee drove, trying his best to hide the broad smile that kept threatening to spread across his face. First he drove her to an area on the outskirts of the city, renowned for its high levels of crime and poor living conditions. The look on her face was a picture and Lee could tell he was pushing her patience to the limit.

"Lee, what is going on?! You don't really expect me to live here do you? Anywhere would be better than here!"

"Well, yes it might have a bad reputation, but you get so much more for your money here. You can get a 3-bed apartment here for the price of a studio further out of town. You could even rent out the 2

other bedrooms for a bit of extra cash." Lee said, biting his lip to stop

himself from laughing.

"No. Just… no. What is next?"

Lee feigned a frustrated sigh and continued driving away from

the city. He spoke about other options, each as ridiculous as the last,

pushing Jennifer to the limit.

"Well there is one last place we could go to, if you're sure none

of these others are suitable?" he said, staring straight ahead of him,

knowing that one look and she would guess what he was up to.

"Sure. Let's just get it over with and go for some lunch. This is

exhausting!" Jennifer was so disappointed. The day had gone from bad

to worse and she was beginning to feel genuinely concerned that Lee

was trying to get rid of her. She just didn't know where all this had come

from. She thought they were stronger than ever.

As she looked out of the window of the car she noticed that

they were driving into a familiar area. Lee pulled into his own drive and turned to face her.

"What about this place? I hear the rent is really low and the landlord is pretty good looking," he said with a cheeky wink.

Her brows furrowed as she looked from the house to Lee and back again. She so desperately wanted to believe that this meant what she hoped it meant, but something stopped her from saying it out loud.

"Jennifer. Will you move in with me?" the cheeky twinkle in his eye was quickly replaced with one of the most genuine smiles she had ever seen.

"Oh Lee! You really fooled me with all this driving around! You drive me mad! Of course I'll move in with you!" She bent across the front of the car and into his arms, her insides filling with excitement at this next step.

Although initially Lee had been unsure as to whether they were ready for a move like this, as they had only been together for less than year, after thinking it through thoroughly, he could see no real reason against it. Ultimately this was the person that he wanted to spend all his time with. The only thing holding him back was the secret of his power, but that was a matter for another time. Together they walked into the house, Jennifer now seeing it with new eyes and almost running into the kitchen to make them both some lunch.

Lee instinctively reached for his phone to tell his brother the news. Tom would no doubt be shocked at this new development and he couldn't wait for his response. But the phone rang out, with no response from Tom.

What was once a rare occurrence was now becoming regular. Before, Tom would always answer Lee's calls, unless he was on duty, but lately Lee could never get hold of him and when he did it was never for long. The pair saw each other less and less and it played on his mind and today it really began to worry him. All he wanted was to share this happy news with the three most important people in his entire life.

*

During holidays Lee would normally return home accompanied by Tom to spend time with their father, going every so often to the cabin that their father brought them to as kids to teach them all their hunting and tracking skills. Lee had even begun to bring Jennifer with him, now that they lived together. Philip always kept a watchful eye over the relationship he had with Jennifer, wanting to keep his son protected and safe. He would read her body language towards him, often when they sat in the car as they arrived in his house for a visit he would watch from inside the house, being sure to remain unseen. Normally the two only ever showed affection. But one time he stood and watched them pull in. They were arguing and Lee seemed upset with what he was hearing. Philip feared Lee was being asked about his powers and was about to go out to cause a distraction for his son. He made his way to the front door and slowly opened it. By the time he opened the door wide enough to peep out he could see Jennifer throwing her arms around Lee and comforting him. Lees face changed and all that could be seen on his face was a look of contentment. Seeing this, Philip closed the door still unseen by the young couple in the car and disappeared back into the house.

He decided that rather than keeping an eye on Jennifer he would in fact try to get to know her a little better. Philip called Lee aside asking if he could go the market and pick up some things, telling him he was going to teach Jennifer how to fish. The prospect of Philip teaching her this was amusing to him.

"Good luck with that, I can't see her baiting a hook!" Philip laughed as he knew when Lee was a boy this was an arduous task that took Philip hours to teach him.

"If I could teach you, I can teach Jennifer."

Lee left Philip to do as he planned.

Jennifer sat in the cabin turning the pages of an old battered book with the spine broken and didn't hear Philip walking in. Peering across the top of the book she was greeted by him holding 2 fishing rods. Bemused as to what he wanted and thinking, *He couldn't possibly want to go fishing with me, I can't even fish*, Philip declared, "Come on, we have a job to do."

Jennifer was mystified by this. "What job?"

"We are going to catch dinner!" Philip countered.

Jennifer simply rose the palm of her hand to her forehead head. Rubbing it slightly, she could only muster the words, "Oh god." But never being shy of a challenge she got up and left with Philip.

Ambling down to the waterfront, Philip carried most of the gear and Jennifer simply carried her rod in hand. When they got there Philip took the rod from Jennifer's hand and slowly showed her how to tie the best knot in the line. Then undoing the same knot and handing her back the rod, he told her, "You can't learn by looking, you learn by doing!"

To his happy amusement, Jennifer retied the knot exactly as he had shown her. "Well I'll be..." proclaimed Philip, "It took Lee a long time to master that knot. In fact, it took me a long time and all. You just did that in your first attempt!"

Jennifer felt a sense of achievement with this and allowed Philip to bait the hook. Not wanting to turn her against the prospect of fishing he did this for her without asking her to handle maggots. She watched as he then baited his own hook and moved closer towards the water. Philip showed her how the mechanics on the rod worked and cast his lure into the water. Propping his rod on a small stand, keeping his line elevated, he turned to once again show Jennifer how to cast her line.

As he turned he was met with the whizzing noise of her line being fired from her reel, both surprised and impressed at her progress, he sat on the bank and watched his own line.

Jennifer sat beside him and the two began something neither of them had done before; they had a conversation just the two of them, without Lee or Tom around.

Mostly sticking to the topic of Lee, Philip was curious to see how much she knew about him and if possible about his secret.

The two danced around the topic and spoke only in pleasantries until Jennifer said something that struck a reaction from Philip that neither had expected.

"Sometimes I get the feeling Lee thinks he doesn't belong here."

"He doesn't," Philip answered.

Jennifer sat there kind of shocked by what Philip had said and asked, "How can you say that about your son?"

Watching him take a deep breath he exhaled for what seemed a very long time; he owed her an explanation to what had just slipped out. Composing his thoughts, he explained himself.

"Lee doesn't know this, but he had a sister." Jennifer's eyes opened wide as this revelation hit. "The reason he doesn't know is very simple, you know the circumstances in which he was born. He lost his mother on the same day which affects him to this day. It has to! But before Josephine had Lee she was expecting a little girl. Tom was too young to remember. She miscarried midway through her pregnancy. If she'd have gone full term, then Lee would not have been born. She would have still been pregnant when he was conceived."

Jennifer, uncomfortable hearing this, as Lee didn't even know, was unsure how to process it. Philip could see this. "Imagine how he would feel."

Jennifer asked, "Why are you telling me this? "

"I don't really know, but I am not asking you to keep secrets. You can tell him if you want. I wanted to so many times, but chose not to."

"Why haven't you?" Jennifer asked.

"Simple. Just because something has to be said, doesn't mean it has to be heard. He has gone through enough without me adding to it. He will feel like he doesn't belong and I feel that despite the world trying to keep him out, he found a way. And he always will. I am not sure about life after death, but I know his life more than anyone else's, even my own, will count."

Jennifer processed the trust he had just placed in her. "I

have my own feelings on life after death…" She paused to gauge his interest and seeing it was there she went on. "My father died when I was young and in part I felt responsible." Hiding the fact, she felt solely responsibly she went on. "It was and is the hardest thing I have ever had to come to terms with and for a long time I struggled. But one day I was in school and we were learning about far away planets and one little fact helped in ways no one can imagine. Kepler 22b is a planet that scientists think can sustain life. An interesting fact, but not the one I am talking about. If you or I were on Kepler 22b right now and we looked back at earth, we would see dinosaurs! This is that fact that has comforted me."

Philip didn't understand to correlation between the fact and Jennifer's comfort and had to ask, "Why?"

"Simply put, if there is a point in the universe where I can go and look back and see dinosaurs then surely there is an infinite amount of points where I can go and see my father being born, going for his first day to school, meeting my mother, teaching me how to ride a bike and, sadly, an infinite amount of points where I can go and watch him die. It comforts me to know that these places exist, and there is no denial of this. It is a solid fact. But one more fact remains, sadly I will never be able to go there."

This incredibly deep and profound thought hit Philip deeper than anything had in such a long time. Struggling to put into words how he felt he let the thought flow through him.

Eventually gearing up to say something, he was cut short by the float on the end of Jennifer's line disappearing under the water. Jumping up excitedly and grabbing her rod she shrieked at Philip. "What do I do?" Talking her through exactly what she was to do, Philip helped her land her first fish and that night's dinner.

Lee returned to the cabin to find it still empty, as he stepped back onto the porch he was greeted by Philip carrying all the equipment and by Jennifer with dinner in hand.

"Oh my god, you actually caught something. It took me ages to ever catch anything!"

Jennifer ran up placed her lips on his and said, "I hope you are good at cleaning fish." All three laughed as Lee took the fish inside to prepare. Jennifer stopped before entering the cabin and turned to Philip. She didn't have to speak, but each offered the other a subtle nod and that was all they had to say. They knew that the other would keep the conversation private as they didn't want to affect Lee's happiness.

CHAPTER TEN

A few weeks after the trip to the cabin Jennifer had to stay late at work to do a stock take in the coffee shop. Lee decided to surprise her with a nice romantic meal, spending hours working in the kitchen on what he hoped to be something special for the two of them. Jennifer was always the one looking after him, so he was looking forward to the opportunity to do something nice for her.

Time passed and Jennifer was late. Aware she should be back but feeling no sense of panic he continued to prep the food in the kitchen. He heard the front door open, which was not unusual, but the slam that followed it was. Walking into the sitting room expecting to see Jennifer coming his way, he was only met by her disappearing shadow as she went straight into the bedroom. Following her in, he asked, "Are you ok? Did something happen?"

Looking back at Lee through tear-filled eyes, all Jennifer could muster was, "They took it," and she broke down crying. Lee rushed over and threw his hands around her. "Who took what?"

Choked up and emotional Jennifer needed to compose herself to answer Lee. "I was mugged, and they took my locket. It's the only thing I have left from him."

Lee both saddened and angered asked once more, "Your father's locket?"

Jennifer whimpered, "Yes." and broke down again.

Panicked, Lee pleaded, "Did they hurt you?"

"Not physically," she answered.

"Did they take your phone?" Jennifer was unable to answer. "Please Jennifer, did they take your phone?"

Confused Jennifer answered, "Yes, but I don't care about that."

Lee stood up, walked over to his laptop and opened it, his fingers furiously tapped at the keyboard and his eyes were transfixed on the screen.

Jumping up and proclaiming, "I got them now!" He grabbed his coat and disappeared out the door. Jennifer didn't understand what Lee was doing and felt hurt that he left her when she needed him the most. She would never have done this to him. Not moving from their bed Jennifer was emotionally drained and just lay there for hours, falling in and out of sleep.

Night time set in and Lee was nowhere to be seen when the house phone rang. Unable to regain her strength she let it ring out. The ringing only stopped long enough for the person on the other end to punch in the number again. Once more Jennifer did not answer. The phone rang a third time, heartbroken and drained Jennifer pulled herself up from under the sheets and picked up the phone. When she answered she was met by a solid questioning voice, "Is this Jennifer Patzner?

"Ehh yes," Jennifer replied and before she had the

opportunity to question the man on the other end of the line, he spoke.

"You need to come to St. James hospital, Lee Sopota is here. He is ok, but he is asking for you."

Panic set in as Jennifer grabbed her coat and ran straight out the door, jumped in the car and left for the hospital. Jennifer abandoned her car right at the entrance to the hospital. She ran to the reception where an unhelpful nurse pointing to the elevator. "The ER is in the basement." Jennifer jumped in the elevator banging on the buttons as the door closed and made her way down. She ran to the counter and asked, "Where is Lee?" The man who spoke to her on the phone was sitting behind the counter and asked, "Are you Jennifer?"

"I am, where is Lee?"

"It's ok, there is no panic, he is fine." The man said reassuringly. "He only has some bruising and a few cuts along with a couple of cracked ribs."

"Cracked ribs?" Jennifer shrieked, "How is that fine?" before the man could answer she demanded, "I need to see him!"

The man came out from behind the desk and said, "No problem, follow me." Jennifer did as the man asked. Walking down the corridor he said, "We had a call from a local drug house that there was a disturbance and we needed to send an ambulance. He really is very lucky; I don't know why someone like him would be in a place like that."

Rounding a corner, Jennifer could see Lee sitting in a chair being attended to by a young doctor. She ran up to him throwing her arms around him once more seeking reassuring comfort. "Are you ok? What happened?" she squeezed Lee a little too tight and he winced with pain.

The doctor said, "You will have to go easy on this fella, he has been through quite an ordeal." He handed Lee a painkiller and some water. "Take these and get some rest," and he left the room.

Jennifer waited for the doctor to leave and demanded from

Lee, "What the hell?"

Lee simply opened his hand and inside there was the locket. "Be more careful with it next time," and laughed, although it was cut short by pain.

Jennifer was visibly shaken by what was happening, "Why would you risk yourself for a locket?"

"It was never a risk, I was never going to lose," he proclaimed.

"But what if you did? I don't know what your power is but how can you expect to beat everyone?" she asked.

His lip curved and he answered, "Well I always have." Reaching out his hand he wiped away a tear from her cheek declaring, "Look Jennifer, I will never stand by while someone I love gets wronged. It's not in my nature. I don't bow down before bullies. Not now, not ever. But the thing you need to trust is that I am smart about it. If there was even a remote chance I would have not got your locket and got back to you in one piece, I would not have taken the risk."

Accepting this, Jennifer asked, "Will I call your father?"

Emphatically Lee responded, "No! Let's just go home."

CHAPTER ELEVEN

Growing comfortable in his life with Jennifer, Lee failed to see that his brother's life was beginning to unravel. Tom was growing distant from him and his family and eventually stopped coming to share the holidays with them. This new routine did not sit well with Lee and Philip, so after some discussion Lee decided the pair would pay his brother a visit.

The two drove to Tom's apartment, but his brother was not to be found. Lee, knowing Tom, understood that the most likely place for him to be was in his father's cabin. It was also a good place to go if a person didn't want to be found as it was secluded and private and paired with Tom's survival skills it was, for the most part, self-sufficient.

They went to the cabin where they found the door ajar. Philip looked at Lee.

"Well at least we know he's here."

Pushing the door, he went inside and Lee followed. The first thing that hit Lee was the stale smell. It smelled like someone had been there drinking for days. Lee looked over to the sink and it was full of dirty dishes and surrounded by empty beer cans. His eyes scanned the room for any signs of his brother. Lee looked over to the table and there was a man doubled over asleep, surrounded by more empty beers cans. Lee thought to himself, *this could not be Tom* as he had never seen him in that kind of state before, but Lee's loyalty to his brother was wrong. It was in fact Tom and he was still drunk.

This was not something either of them expected from the highly disciplined soldier that Tom was. Lee sat and spoke softly and candidly to his brother, a man who he truly looked up to, with the knowledge his brother only had his best intentions at heart and being able to trust him with any secret. Tom began to speak, opening up to Lee all about his true role in the army, the things that the government were doing in order to maintain the balance of peace. He told him about his reconnaissance missions and what they were truly in aid of, speaking of how the government really dealt with crime factions loyal to the Old World Alliance, with a bloody and cruel iron fist.

Anyone who stood in opposition to the world treaty would be suppressed in the name of a higher peace. Before the government wiped out its enemies it would perform experiments on the individuals in order to learn their weaknesses so the government could better quash future uprisings and maintain the balance of power.

Lee had long suspected that the reason the stories of this nature got pulled from his newspaper was governmental interference. All of Tom's stories then culminated into one; the government used Tom to recon all the enemies of the states, then used a weapon against the opposing factions to eliminate them.

"I never knew what the weapon was, until one night on a mission I got delayed from his extraction and witnessed the army using the weapon. What I viewed was not what I expected. The weapon wasn't a *what* it was a *who*."

He went on to explain further. "I viewed the target compound for about six hours to get an accurate and detailed report of all inside and I also had to make sure that the main target was inside. After five hours I reported back to base that there was a positive ID on the target. I also stated that the target's families were in residence, including women and children..."

"After waiting an hour I radioed back to base that they were clear to engage. As I maneuvered my way to the extraction point, I found myself pinned down between a tower and a patrol vehicle, which had stopped to check the perimeter.

Being careful to go unseen I hid in a shallow drain on a hill overlooking the compound. It was this delay and vantage point that allowed me to see what was going to happen, being able to view the courtyard to the compound and the buildings that over looked it. Along the perimeter I was able to see the two watch towers that had guards concealed within. It was then I heard a large explosion, as one of the towers burst into violent flames and the guards within screeched with agony from the flames burning them alive. But the screams were short lived when another explosion echoed out from the other tower. This time there were no screams and the compound fell silent for a moment that seemed to last an eternity.

I stayed still and concealed myself as I waited for events to unfold. The patrol vehicle that had halted my withdrawal from the area was now speeding in the direction of the explosions to valiantly confront whatever had caused the chaos below, freeing me to withdraw. I chose to watch events unfold rather than to make haste with my exit. Sirens broke the intolerable silence and I viewed a lone masked soldier enter the compound. He was scouting and wreaking havoc to all inside…"

"Do you remember the stories Dad used to tell us about the leap, and how the first kids affected would wear masks and costumes to hide their identities? This soldier looked something like how you would imagine them to look, but he could not have been mistaken for a hero…"

Tom continued on through glistening eyes. "I watched this single individual lay waste to all in front of him, he seemed to grow stronger and faster with every person he faced in combat. He laid waste to the entire compound and moved with a stealthy determination. Some of the enemy soldiers laid down their arms in the face of this superior force, but this did not stop the individual from executing all inside. Innocent or guilty, the individual showed no bias and murdered all inside without proper proof of guilt.

In my recon report I viewed at least fifty operatives within the compound, along with the main target and his entire family and none of them stood a chance against this individual's attack. The last thing I heard before a deafening silence was the cries of children ringing out…"

Tom was a highly intelligent person and knew that the sort of concealed dynamism that this one masked individual possessed would have to be unstable. As he spoke he let his feelings known for what he had witnessed.

"Murdering innocent people that I swore to protect goes against everything that I hold true to me, so I resolved to investigate further.

After a few weeks of researching into the 'weapon' with no significant breakthrough, I uncovered some highly classified files on a ghost server in a secret basement in the base where I'm stationed and learned that the weapon was filed as Project K. Also, every individual who took part in the development of Project K met with a tragic end. It gave me chills and thinking about it now only adds to it."

Tom told his brother, "As I read the files I learned how Project K operated, that this one individual was able to absorb the powers of those he fought and permanently fuse their energy with his whilst not absorbing their weaknesses. Making him effectively immune to any attack an enemy could strike onto him.

I also found files, which were buried by his superiors, that showed that Project K was unstable and had a tendency to go rogue. By targeting non-threatening individuals whose powers were strong, Project K was able to absorb their energy and make him stronger. The files also contained the subsequent cover ups to hide the fact that Project K was targeting civilians."

Spooked by seeing this, Tom opted to copy the files and approach his old commanding officer with the information; the now Second Class Sergeant McKay. Despite their strained relationship he remained a man Tom had served with for the past five years and a man Tom trusted with his life. The two men met in a bar that soldiers regularly visited. They shared a few stories and a few beers and spoke of missions that the two had undertaken in previous years. Tom had been dancing around the topic of what he wanted to say to McKay for a while and eventually plucked up the courage and told McKay his story.

He told him about the delay on the mission and about the masked individual, the secret basement and about the ghost server. Giving McKay a copy of the files, he told him they were the only copy as he didn't want them falling into the wrong hands. McKay seemed sceptical of the information he was being given, but would look into it further and promised to keep Tom's identity as the source of the information secret.

Tom also told Lee that this was the last time he saw McKay and that after that he was immediately transferred out of the base and no one in his company saw him again. Tom began to worry for his own safety and told Lee that this is why he had been visiting the family less and less; as a measure to protect them from any potential backlash. He explained how he had become increasingly paranoid that his apartment was being monitored and relocated to the cabin, which no one outside the family had knowledge of. He also knew that no one would be able to approach it without his knowledge.

By this stage Tom was beginning to sober up, thanks in part to the strong coffee his father had brewed for him. Lee interrogated him about the story in order to measure his brothers' safety concerns. He asked if it was possible that he had been seen entering the basement, but Tom assured him counter measures were taken. Lee also asked if Tom passed the information to anyone else, and Tom told him that the only times he had spoken about Project K was to McKay.

"Was the copy you gave McKay in fact the only copy you

made?"

Tom hesitated before answering and Lee knew from this that he had in fact made another copy for safe keeping and that there was two possibly scenarios at play: 1. The army did not learn of Tom's involvement in un-earthing the files or 2. They knew he was involved and were monitoring him in order to learn the whereabouts of the files and assess the threat level that Tom posed.

Tom said that they would not be able to find the files and if something happened to him that the only people who would be able to find them would be Lee and Philip. They all agreed that the safest place for Tom to stay was in the cabin. Knowing this, Lee and Philip decided to return to their homes. Before leaving, his brother called out to him.

"Lee, even a broken clock is right twice a day..."

This comment left Lee confused as he searched his mind for a reason for this statement.

"Don't worry about that just now, I'm sure you will figure it out..." Tom smiled warmly to his younger brother and turned away from him, allowing him to leave.

CHAPTER TWELVE

Jennifer met Lee as he was coming in the door with her usual smile and soft kiss and for that brief moment the anxiety Lee felt about his brother's safety disappeared, but as Jennifer took her lips away from his, the overwhelming anxiousness he had for his brother began to rise again. Jennifer asked him what was wrong and Lee willingly explained, knowing he needed to ease Jennifer's mind.

"Tom is in danger, but I can't really go into details of what is happening, as y o u r safety could be put at risk and this is something I just can't do. I cannot and will not put you in harm's way." He kissed her again, held her reassuringly close and spoke softly in her ear. "Let's go to bed." So they did.

Lee returned to work as usual, editing all the stories of interest over the following weeks, but on one day a particular story caught his eye. It was titled *Local Football Hero Goes Missing*. It was about a young student, who was a college football prospect from a small farming village outside the city, missing in strange circumstances. This story struck a note with Lee, so he decided to go back through the pulled stories from the last eighteen months. He went to see how many similar stories there were. It wasn't long before a pattern began to emerge; the pattern included the targeting of people with vulnerable backgrounds, such as young people and old people from disadvantaged and rural areas.

They were all targeted in similar circumstances.

The details given to the authorities at the time matched the masked individual that Tom had seen attacking the compound. Lee quickly figured that the reason the stories were being pulled was because the perpetrator was a valuable member of the armed forces within the United New World and was being protected by his superior command. Lee went to share this information with his brother, wanting to get his advice about what they should do next. As he drove he seemed to hit every red light on the way and a traffic jam, frustrating Lee. The more he wanted to hurry the slower the traffic went. Eventually he relaxed and accepted that all he could do was wait for the traffic to relent. But by the time he reached the cabin, much to Lee's dismay and distress, he found it to be empty.

There was no sign of his brother, no sign of a struggle and no sign of any foul play. Lee being Lee and knowing his brother, knew something was seriously wrong. He sat for a moment with the feeling that something wasn't right, knowing 'if something isn't right then it's wrong'. Applying his logical thinking to the scenario in hand, he looked around and saw there was no sign of a struggle, which meant that Tom went willingly with whoever came for him. For if Tom put up a struggle, given his strength there probably wouldn't have been much left intact in the cabin. Lee also knew if Tom was to be taken, given a chance he would leave him a clue.

So pulling a chair from by the door he sat it in the middle of the room and scanned everything. At first glance nothing seemed out of place. Taking a second scan of the room and still seeing nothing wrong, but trusting his instincts, he sat with the idea that maybe what Tom left was not something that's out of place, but something that should be there.

The first thing Lee saw was the ashtray on the table. Tom did not smoke, but Lee knew that if needed he would have a cigarette so he could give Lee and Philip a timeframe of when he left the cabin. Lee felt the ash and there was still a little heat in it. Had he not been delayed in traffic he may have made it to the cabin in time to help his brother.

Lee sat back down and looked for more indications as to what happened, becoming conscious of the fact that the big grandfather clock had been fully wound up, but the time on the clock was unchanged. The clock was stuck at 1.48. This time was familiar to him, but he did not know why. He recalled the words Tom had left him with.

"Even a broken clock it right twice a day..."

At the time these words seemed cryptic, but now Lee comprehended that he was telling him where to look. Carefully he opened the glass door that covered the clock face, only to hear something inside the clock fall. He peered into the bottom of the clock to see if he could see what. It was too dark to make out any distinct objects, so running into the kitchen he grabbed a torch from the cupboard underneath the sink.

Returning to the clock he lit the torch. It struggled to ignite the filament in the bulb, but after gentle persuasion by hitting it with his other hand, the torch lit up and he shone it into the darkness in the clock. He saw a black pouch and reaching his hand in, he retrieved it.

Carefully he carried it to the table by the window and began to inspect it. Opening it carefully, he removed the contents for examination. From a quick inspection he gathered it to be a hard drive from a computer, but he had never seen one like this before.

It was the same size as a normal drive, but the markings on it were very different to any he had seen before. It appeared to be military grade technology. He ran to his car and grabbed his laptop to connect the device and learn what secrets were hidden inside. Swiftly he booted up his laptop and connected it all in a hurried panic. Just before the device powered up, it struck him how easily this process had unfolded.

Lee's face crumpled; his brother would always fail-safe anything of importance. Choosing to re-examine the device; carefully, he opened it and discovered a circuit board missing. Lee exhaled a breath of relief, certain that if plugged in the device would then most likely have corrupted any information on it and his brother would have been lost. Searching every part of the cabin to find the missing circuit board, he could not find it or any clue as to its location. Lee knew only one person knew his brother's thinking as well as he did. With that in mind he left the cabin.

Lee took the device and drove to his father's house to show him what he had found. Met by his father who had been tidying up the back yard, Philip's first words to Lee were, "Any news on Tom?" His voice held concern that his casual words could not conceal. Lee turned to his father.

"Come into the house and I will tell you the whole story." After hearing the whole story, Philip maintained his usual calm, but insisted they he take a look at the cabin himself, determined to not miss anything. Together they drove to the cabin in silence, neither wishing to speculate about what might have happened.

They entered and at first Philip could not see anything missing or out of place.

"They took Tom, and he let them take him. Look, there is nothing here out of place, not a thing. You and I know what Tom would have done if he had put up a fight." This was chilling for Philip to hear, as he knew Tom only went because he didn't have a choice and this was scarier to him than if he had entered a room that Tom turned over with anger. It was unturned by fear.

Lee reaffirmed what his father was thinking.

"Tom went willingly, this panics me! Knowing him as we do I know that he would have left a clue for us to find him."

He went on to explain about the clock not working and the device hidden at the bottom and how only at the last second did he remember that Tom would have protected the information held on the device and how upon further examination he opened it to see a circuit board missing.

"…but there was no clue as to where the circuit board

was." Lee concluded, dragging his hands through his hair as the weight of this felt heavy on his shoulders. Philip was equally stuck in finding an answer to where his son could have hidden the circuit.

Recalling the time on the clock, he queried the meaning of it. "Does the time 1.48 have any significance to us? I know it does, I just can't remember why..."

Philip took a moment to think over the scenario his son described to him and the numbers he had quoted to him. With sorrowful understanding, his father sighed.

"Yes, but it's not what you think. It's not 1.48. It's 13.48 on the 24hr clock." Philip paused and took another breath, looking his son in the eye, he instructed him. "Get your coat and come with me."

He did as his father asked, taking his coat and following him outside.

They got into Philip's car and drove south out of the town.

About 4 kilometres out his father turned left up a small country road. Driving for another few minutes they then pulled in.

"I haven't taken you here since you were a child. It was too difficult for me; in fact, I am surprised your brother remembered."

Lee peered out the window at something that resonated like a memory he had lost and couldn't place. Philip gestured to him, "Follow me." Lee did as his father asked, despite this being very strange to him. They strolled up along a wall, gazing in across the top Lee saw that on the other side was a small graveyard. With this a memory of this place began to come back to Lee.

Reliving the last time he was here, that day had sat in perfect silence much like today. He could see birds and a small stream that ran down the centre of the graveyard. Despite knowing they were making noise, the day remained perfectly silent. Lee walked two steps behind his father as a nervous child would; he trusted his father's direction completely.

Stopping, closing his eyes he began to speak.

"Love is patient. Love is kind. It does not envy. It does not boast. It is not proud. It is not rude. It is not self-seeking. It is not easily angered. It keeps no record of wrongs. Love does not delight in evil, but rejoices with the truth. It always protects, always trusts, always hopes, and always perseveres. Love never fails…"

With that he took a step to the right allowing his son to see what was in front of him. It was his mother's grave. Philip looked at his son in contemplation.

"Corinthians 13, verses 4- 8, 13.48; this is what your mother read to me on the day we were married."

Lee's eye went back to the grave where the words of scripture his father had quoted were engraved on a headstone accompanied by his mother's name, date of birth and along with this, he read his own birthday.

The two men stood in silence for a moment as they both paid their respects. Philip, to the woman he loved and wanted to spend his life with, but was unable to save, and Lee to the woman that saved him by giving up her life.

Moments passed and the two men slowly began to reconcile the emotions that had been stirring from within them. There was a bunch of plastic flowers in a small brass vase sitting in front of the headstone.

"Your brother left you something. Look in the pot."

Lee removed the flowers from the vase and inspecting inside saw it was full of water.

"A bit unnecessary for plastic flowers, I think..." Philip uttered from behind him, so he removed the vase from his mother's grave and completely tipped the water out and stuck his hand inside to see if there was anything within. There was a small watertight container stuck to the bottom. He removed it, already aware of what the contents were. He presented it to his father to make the discovery. Philip slowly opened the box as Lee was keeping a careful eye to make sure his father didn't damage anything inside. As they both peered into the open box they saw it was in fact the circuit board they were seeking to make the hard drive work. Philip handed it back to Lee and he put it in his inside pocket. The two men paid their final respects to Josephine and left her graveside.

Returning to his apartment that night with the hard drive and the circuit board, Lee carefully opened the drive and reattached the circuit board; then closed it, sealing it once again.

As his laptop booted up, once again he connected the drive to the computer, this time turning it on. As the system loaded, Jennifer came into the room and appealed to him. "What's going on?"

She sat patiently and listened as he told her about the events that had been surrounding Tom and what they had uncovered.

When he finished telling her everything, Jennifer was extremely nervous and uncomfortable with the news.

"I think we should call the police!"

"The people involved were above the police and no one can know what's going on if there is to be any chance of finding my brother."

Lee took Jennifer's hand and looked her in the eyes, reassuring her. "Jenny I need you to trust me on this. It's my brother. He's not only my brother, but he's my best friend and my hero and I need to be the one to find him."

Jennifer conceded to Lee's judgment, knowing him only to ever speak like this when his mind was made up. She wanted to stay to comfort him in his time of need, but appreciated he would not be able to offer up any information. She conceded, "I truly love and trust you. I'll go to bed… Don't be too late." she stood up kissed him on the lips and left the room.

Turning his attention back to the computer that was fully booted at this stage, he began opening the drive on his computer and found all the files that his brother had previously told him about. He spent the whole night reading about Project K and all the related missions. Reading dossiers and reports on everything associated with Project K. He even found all his brother's reconnaissance reports. Buried deep in the files he noticed a folder called *Corinthians*. He opened it and seeing inside there was a video file, he hit play.

What was to happen next both frightened Lee and gave him hope that his brother was safe. It was a video Tom had recorded before he went missing.

The video started with Tom having a sullen look on his face and he began to speak, "Lee if you found this then we both know that I have been taken in. I am still alive for if you are the one to find this it means I haven't given up the location of the device yet, but know this; the people that have me will stop at nothing to get the information on it back. You cannot let this happen, Lee. If they come for me I will go freely because I know what they are capable of and if they send Project K my strength will count for nothing.

So I am relying on you, little brother. You need to blow the lid on what has been going on. Just know that if you do before I can escape they will certainly kill me. And always remember, *trust your gut, it won't lie to you, if something doesn't feel right it's wrong."* The video ended.

Sitting for a few moments and processing what just happened and feeling a combination of physical and emotional exhaustion he looked out the window, seeing the sun had begun to rise. Lee pulled himself upstairs and lay on the bed beside Jennifer for a few moments before his alarm started ringing out. Sleepy eyed and drained, he dragged himself to the shower and freshened up for work. Stashing the device under the floor in the spare room in the apartment, he slid over a chest of drawers to cover it for safekeeping.

When Lee got to work he went to speak to his boss, knowing him to be a good man. But he was unsure as to whether he could trust him fully with the information that his brother had acquired. Bashfully approaching the subject of all the pulled stories and the process that was behind it, Lee's boss Pete Laurie explained. "I am required to e-mail all stories for approval to a particular address," he showed Lee the email address.

It was a government assigned email.

"Only on one occasion did I run a story without prior approval. It was a late breaking story but I was unable to get approval in time so I just ran it…"

He explained. "The story was about a pension scheme in one of the regional airlines and was of no major interest or consequence to anything that would affect the government, but the fact that it was run without approval meant I was severely reprimanded."

Pete turned to Lee, "It wasn't always like this and if I had my choice it would never be like this again."

Lee approached the topic of publishing another unapproved story, but this one was big and would be a game changer for everything to come after. Pete got up and closed the door to his office, turned to him and demanded, "What kind of game changer?”

Lee replied, “corruption and cover ups to the highest levels of The United New World government…”

Pete stated, “I categorically will have nothing to do with anything of the sort; I can’t risk it. There are too many people and jobs depending on me!”

Lee realised his mistake, apologised and tried to make an excuse to leave.

Pete followed up with, “I think you misunderstand me Lee, I will have nothing to do with it as it's too risky for me to get involved again, but I won't stop you from sneaking into my office and adding the story to the final edit…”

Lee was relieved to now have a channel to get the story out, but also needed time to try to find his brother.

Thanking Pete and playing for time, Lee said, “I need time to work on the story.” What he really meant was he needed time to find Tom.

"Go home and work on the story, as there are too many prying eyes in the office and all activity is logged. A story like this would be flagged long before it was completed."

CHAPTER THIRTEEN

Lee went home to try to develop a plan to find out where his brother was. Re-reading the files about Project K, and having further studied them and the additional information left to him by Tom, he judged that the most likely place Tom was being held was in the base where he had found the files in the secret bunker.

Fortunately for Lee, within the files Tom provided there were detailed schematics of the bunker. Unfortunately the bunker appeared to be a lot bigger than anticipated. The bunker was the same size as the whole base with only one visible entry point. Therein lay another problem; he had found schematics for the bunker, but not for the base itself, so he would have to find another way to locate the entry point within the base.

The bunker included a full underground training area, medical area and unnamed rooms that appeared to be either cells or an interrogation area. These cells were located at the furthermost point from the entrance to the bunker making them the most likely placc to hold a prisoner; as escape would be near impossible.

The files also contained detailed description of the protocols the security adhered to when within the bunker, Lee needed to get more information as to where exactly on the base the entrance to the bunker was. Knowing that if there was such a large sealed structure underground then there had to be another point of entry, somewhere such as air vents to pump fresh air around the facility.

Packing up the car with all his hunting equipment and hiking gear he began the long drive north to the hills where the base was concealed, unknown to anyone who wasn't privy to such information. Thoughts ran through his mind as he drove and he tried to focus on the task at hand and the road unfolding out before him, but he could not shift the uncomfortable feeling in the pit of his stomach. His brother meant everything to him and he genuinely didn't think that his father could take another loss in the family. He knew that he still felt the loss of his wife acutely, but put on a brave face for the sake of him and Tom. He had to find and rescue Tom for all their sakes.

Driving up an old dirt road Lee met a dead end, where he parked the car and loaded the gear on his back. Strapping to his hip his trusty hunting knife that he had used on the bear many years before, he began his hike into the mountains on foot through the hills to his targeted destination. Armed with his full hunting gear and schematics of the base, he navigated the hills with ease, using the stars as his guide.

The base itself was well hidden and high up in the hills. Lee needed to approach the area from an elevated position on the other side of the ridge overlooking the base. Continuing along the ridge he looked for a good vantage point from which he could gauge the base properly.

Reaching the crest of the hill, he bedded down out of sight, combing the area to see if he could locate the entrance to the bunker underneath the base.

Lee stayed awake the whole night, learning the shift patterns of the guards. They would change position every two hours and they would all take three different positions during a shift.

When the shift ended they would go to the security guards' quarters and sleep. This is how they rotated the shifts at night, with half the guards asleep and half on duty. Lee synchronised his watch to match the change of the guards, still not able to locate the entrance to the bunker.

As the sun came up he tried to sleep a little as fatigue began to grip him. He awoke some hours later to resume monitoring the patterns of the guards. The pattern he noted on the night previous continued during the day, which made no sense to him. "Why would half the guards be sleeping during the day?" he thought to himself. With the arrival of the sun he was also able to see the faces of the guards and was struck by the fact that there were a lot more guards than he noted the night before when they appeared to be dark faceless figures.

Originally evaluating inaccurately that while half were on guard the other half were asleep in the guard's quarters, now it appeared that there were a lot more than half in the quarters at any one time, even more than the quarters could accommodate. Having a hunch that the most likely place for the entrance to the bunker to be hidden was in the guards' quarters, the focus of his attention shifted to this building.

He laid out the schematics of the base on the ground and tried to position it in a way so that it would reflect the layout of the bunker. As the bunker was directly under the base it was easy enough for him to map out the position. He also made careful note of the area above ground, highlighting all possible escape routes. Mapping in his mind where the vehicles were kept, where the highest density of guards were, he considered the most likely escape route should anything go wrong.

With the light of day it was easy for him to see exactly where the guards were positioned. There were seven guarded posts in total and each position had two guards. One post was at the entrance to the base with another two occupying the two towers to the left and the right of the entrance at the corner of the base. There was another based at the entrance to the main building, another was located at the entrance to the supply room and there was a third tower to the rear of the base with two in the tower and two along the back fence to guard the rear of the building.

It also became apparent that each tower had a spotlight, a sharpshooter and a spotter concealed behind a mesh of camouflage.

It was hard to see the movement of these soldiers in day light, but their warm breath against cold air would make it easier to locate and track their movements at night.

Lee carefully compared the bunker schematics against the base that lay in front of him. Deducting that if his brother was being held in the cells as previously considered, it was most likely to be located to the rear of the base near the bottom of the tower.

But from where he was perched, his view of that part of

the area was obstructed by the main building. It was extremely risky for him to enter through the guards' quarters and go unnoticed. Waiting for nightfall, he began to manoeuvre both down and around the hill to position himself at the rear of the base, keeping his distance so he would not be spotted easily.

Lee took up position about five hundred meters away from the fence and gauged the area. He could see at the bottom of the tower there was a large industrial air ventilation unit. Immediately he judged this to be the best potential point of access to the bunker below. To get to this unit he would have to pass through two perimeter fences undetected. It was between these fences that additional guards patrolled on foot.

Lee was fully camouflaged in his hunting gear and as luck would have it, that night was particularly foggy and he was able to mask himself better in the darkness. The fog also helped him hide his warm breath in the cold air. He timed his advance to the back fence so that the tower spotlight was farthest away from him and the patrol guards were in the opposite direction. The point in which he approached the fence was directly beneath the tower so he needed to gain access to the base in total silence. By approaching the fence here, Lee was in a blind spot from the spotlight and could not be seen unless the guards had been alerted to his presence. It also left the shortest distance between him and the ventilation unit. However, he was directly in the path of the two guards on foot patrol.

Reaching the outer fence, he lay at the base of it, camouflaged and undetected. Waiting for the light to pass from left to right, he then removed his wire cutters from their pouch in his trousers and began to cut an opening along the base of the fence. Cutting a length long enough for him to slide underneath with relative ease, he worked his way across the gap between the fences ensuring to stay as low to the ground as possible and making only moves as intended.

Moving towards the internal perimeter fence, the guards were getting closer to his position. Edging his body against the fence the guards were within only a few feet of where he lay.

They began to pass by him when one of them stopped

and turned in the direction of Lee. He quietly gasped, holding his breath thinking he had been spotted, but desperately hoping he hadn't been. The guard began to walk towards him.

Seeing this, he slowly ran his hand down his hip to where his knife was. He also had in his possession a tranquiliser gun, but the effects of the gun wouldn't be instant so in this case he opted for his knife. He gripped the handle and readied it for action, knowing that if seen there was very little chance he would ever make it home to see Jennifer again. He did not know what kind of powers these guards possessed, adding further danger to the situation. Very little ran through Lee's head as survival mode kicked in. The constant battle in his thoughts went silent for a little while. He stopped thinking about Tom's disappearance and Jennifer's worry. He only thought about getting through the next few minutes.

Less than a few paces from the vents with only the fence standing in the way, Lee was so close to getting in unseen and undetected. Lee made himself small on the ground and lay motionless. He was virtually invisible. He would remain so unless the guard had already spotted him or if he trod upon Lee's motionless body.

The guard continued his silent advance towards Lee, but stopped abruptly, planting his boots within spitting distance of Lee's face. So close in fact Lee saw his breath slowly steam up the tip of his left boot. He was careful to control his airflow, fearing the fog would no longer conceal it while the guards were so close.

The guard reached into his pocket to search for something and tilting his head upwards toward the tower and let out a loud whisper. "Psst Jack."

Lee kept his face down, in hopes that the guard would not look down to the ground and spot him. He gripped his knife tightly while trying to figure out in his head what was going on, when he heard a louder whisper, "Psst Jack..." but this time there came a response from up in the tower.

"Yeah, what's up?"

"Throw me down your matches; I need a smoke…" and

with that the guards in the tower dropped a box of matches to the man below. The guard fished out a pack of cigarettes from his pocket and began to light one up. His partner, who was a little further on turned to him, saying, "Man those things will kill you…"

The guard then inhaled deeply from his cigarette, turned away from Lee and slowly started to walk. Lee loosened his grip on the knife and inwardly revelled, thinking, *they nearly did and you have no idea.*

With that Lee began to cut along the bottom of the second fence, again allowing him enough room to pass underneath undetected. From this point it was only a few meters further for him to reach the vents and hopefully an entry point.

He got to the vents undetected; slowly unscrewing the cover to the vent and slipping into it, closing it behind him.

He stopped for a moment to take a breath and think of what was next. Before undertaking this mission Lee planned to get into the base to find the bunker in hopes that Tom was being held there, but he was left with only his instinct as to where within the bunker his brother actually was. Working his way along the vents, slowly lowering himself down the vertical shaft, he used the rope he brought in his pack, and dropped down further and further into the bunker until he reached the bottom.

Here the shaft split in two directions. He decided to go to the right, but after a moment Lee hesitated, peering ahead seeing a long maze of vents that were feeding into the rest of the compound. He sensed this to be wrong, as he had previously deduced the cells to be close to the point where he entered into the vent system. He slowly worked back up the shaft and then headed to the left. Passing down the shaft, carefully checking all the rooms he passed over to look for evidence that his brother was there.

Reaching the end of the vent he found the rooms he had highlighted to himself on the schematics. There were two rows of three cells, hidden from sight in the safe confines of the vents. Lee could see into the cells on one side and was clearly able to see they had no-one inside. This was going to force Lee to take a big risk in making himself visible.

CHAPTER FOURTEEN

As the cells were empty, the doors were left wide open in the first two. Entering either of these would leave minimal cover if a patrol walked by the cells. The third cell door was open, but left ajar so he decided this would be his best point of entry, as the door would offer him some degree of cover in the cell.

There was a vertical drop down the vent into the room, so he secured himself at the top using a rope and slowly lowered himself head first down the shaft to the vent cover. He began to unscrew the cover of the vent and carefully remove it, being sure to not make any noise as he passed through the vent to the ground below. The room he found himself in was dark; the only light illuminating his line of sight came from the light in the corridor outside the cell, which leaked in through the gap in the door and through the small window on the door. The cell was small with only a mattress lying on the floor behind him, in full view of any guard looking through the viewing hatch as they passed by the door on their patrol. There was also a steel washbasin and a stainless steel toilet.

The door into the cell was made of heavy steel with four electrically controlled lock bars and a small window in the centre for the guards to keep an eye on any prisoners. He examined the door and thought to himself, *this door is heavy duty, but I don't think it would hold Tom. If he's locked in here and hasn't escaped, it's only because he's chosen not to...*

He peered out the door, through the gap between it and the wall; from here he could see the three cells that lay adjacent to the one he was in. He could also see down the corridor to where a guard was sitting. The guard seemed to have his feet up, watching a small TV perched on a shelf behind the desk.

This meant that the guard was looking away from where the cells were located and as there was not a recognisable entry point from that direction he had no need to be suspicious of anything from behind him.

Lee needed to assess if in fact his brother was held in any of the other cells. Removing his heavy hiking boots in case they made noise on the ground and alerted the guard to his presence, he opened the door gradually and gently made his way out.

Stepping up to the first cell, which was the furthest away from the guard, he spied into the cell and took a survey of everything he saw. The room was dark, too dark to assess if his brother was inside. But while staring in through the window, his eyes adjusted to the darkness, and gauged there was nobody in the room.

Calmly and deliberately he moved onto the next cell, being careful to choose where to place his feet. Each time he took a pace forward he would look up to see if the guard had been alerted to any movement from over his shoulder, being mindful to control his breathing, for if the guard turned around he would clearly see Lee standing behind him.

There was nowhere for him to hide between where he stood and the desk that separated him from the guard. Being unsure of the guard's power added further danger to this undertaking. Making it to the second door, he again sought to confirm if his brother was in the cell or not.

As his eyes adjusted to the darkness inside he saw that there was the figure of a man inside. Unable to see if the features of the person inside were the same as his brother, as the person lying in the room had their back to the door, he raised his hand to make a small noise on the glass to get the attention of whoever was inside.

Pulling his hand back he began to slowly release it towards the glass. He interrupted his own movement just as contact was about to be made with the window and paused for a moment to think. If he tapped the window the guard could be alerted to his presence and if he was lucky enough not to, and the person inside was not his brother, they would certainly make a noise and bring the attention of the guard towards the cells. Instead he chose to examine the third and final cell.

Tentatively Lee backed away from where he was standing.

Walking in the direction of the third cell, he was careful to stay low, so as to not cast too long of a shadow ahead of him towards the guard, who was still engrossed in watching his inaudible, small and fuzzy TV. Every so often the guard would let out a chuckle at the programme he was watching.

Again he made very deliberate movements, being careful to focus his breathing so he didn't make a noise over that of the TV, reaching the final cell undetected. Every ounce of his being was focused on finding his brother and getting out of that place. He didn't want to be in there for a second longer than he had to be, but he knew that he had to do it right. As these thoughts past through his mind, his head instinctively twitched a fraction, as if to expel them from his head through motion alone, for he couldn't handle the reality of a world without his brother and thinking about it wasn't going to get any of them anywhere.

Breathing in and trying to remember the relaxation techniques that his father had taught him, he forced his mind back to the task at hand. He was still bent down to avoid casting a shadow. Extending his legs and straightening his back, he looked through the window to see if anyone was inside.

The light from behind Lee shone in through the window onto the floor inside and the first thing he saw was a pair of boots on the ground. So he had at least discovered that there was someone inside. The silhouette cast by the shadow of Lee's head obstructed his view of the person who lay inside.

Angling his body so the light passed over his shoulder revealed the person that lay therein, as the light passed over him he was able to see the features of a man that he had loved his entire life, a man he would risk all to save. Lee had finally found Tom.

He raised his hand and waved it in front of the light to wake his brother from his sleep, the breaking light got Tom's attention and slowly he began to wake. Tom, confused as to what was going on, was fighting off the symptoms of a deep sleep. Seeing the shadow cast by his brother trying to get his attention, he slowly got up from the bed and walked towards the door.

With every small half-awake half-asleep movement he

made, he woke a little more. Through the light he saw the silhouette of a person beckoning him begin to fade and the features of the man in the door began to come clear.

Firstly he saw eyes that he had known for what seemed to him to be forever, then a furrowed look of fear that he had only seen a few times. In fact, the last time he saw that look of apparent fear and relief was not since they came face to face with the bear, all those many years before. The face gawking out at Lee was that of a man confused, scared and excited.

Before any explanation was given to Tom or before he had a chance to seek one, Lee raised his hand to his face and placed his finger in front of his lips, signalling Tom to remain quiet.

No sooner had he made this gesture to his brother than a high-pitched screech rang out from between Lee and the guard, who sat only a few paces away. Lee's eyes opened wide as he looked in at his brother and any relief that he had held instantly drained to terror.

Tom's expression reflected that of his younger brother who was risking everything to find him. Lee dropped to the ground and using his entire body he pushed off the wall and slid along the polished ground in the direction of the guard. He pushed his body tight up against the security desk, which hid him from the guard's line of sight.

The screech sounded again, this time followed by a voice, "Ericson come in, over." The security guard remained motionless, before there was time for any reaction from the guard the radio sounded again, "Ericson do you copy, over..." the guard swung round on his chair and lifted the radio that sat on the desk just over Lee's head.

Lee listened for a response.

"Yea this is Ericson, what you want?!" a voice declared back to him in a disapproving tone.

"Ericson this is command, you never checked in, over…" Before replying Ericson murmured to himself, "What is there to check in…" But his reporting came out clearly. "Prisoners secured, all clear…" turning his back away from Lee, once again he looked at his programme. As he turned, the voice on the radio barked.

"Ericson it's your job to check in, not my job to ask, over…"

Again Ericson murmured, "Yeah, yeah, yeah…"

Lee composed himself and reached his hand slowly across his belt and removed the tranquiliser gun from where it was sitting on his belt. Taking it up to his chest and pausing for focus, he took a few slow deep breaths.

Beginning to position himself to neutralise any threat posed by guard, he got to his feet while remaining crouched and hidden behind Ericson. Raising his body up over the desk, gripping and stretching out the gun in front of him, he held Ericson in his sights and slowly pulled down on the hammer. As he did this the TV fell silent in a lull of activity and the noise was plain for Ericson to hear.

Spinning around in the chair he was sitting in he saw a startled Lee looking back at him. Lee fired one round straight at him, thinking there was ample time to hit him before he could react.

To Lee's confusion all he hit was an empty chair and Ericson was nowhere to be seen. A flabbergasted Lee stood up and looked down over the desk to see if Ericson had sought coverage behind the chair, he had not. Lee instantly grabbed the radio from off the desk and slipped it into his pocket, and turned around to search the area to see where Ericson went. As he turned around he found Ericson standing in front of him with a menacing look in his eyes. He quickly surmised that Ericson had one of three abilities. Either Ericson was a teleporter, had the gift of speed or he could turn invisible. Quickly Lee ruled out invisibility, as the dart he fired at him would have still hit him even if he had been able to bend light around his body. So he was either a teleporter, which was very rare or possessed the capability of speed.

Ericson just stood there and waited for Lee to make his move. He raised the tranquiliser gun from his hip, but by the time he raised it to shoulder level an immense impact landed on the side of his face and he fell to the ground. Stunned he looked up again at Ericson who was in the exact same position. Ericson smirked back at Lee and simply stated, "Faster than a speeding bullet, and certainly faster than you..."

No sooner had the words reached Lee's ears than yet another tremendous blow impacted on his face. This time Lee was left dazed by the blow and looking onto the ground below him he saw a steady stream of blood flow from his face.

Tom had been watching these events unfold from inside his cell and as soon as he saw that Lee was in trouble he stood back from the door, clenched his fists and with a grimace upon his face he planted his right foot on the ground. He leaned back, raised his left foot and with all his might kicked the steel door that was in front of him. With one colossal wallop he kicked the steel door clean off the wall, taking a large chunk out of the wall as well.

He stuck his head out through the door and Ericson was quick to stick it back in by landing a blow square on his chin. But as the strike landed and Ericson went to move away from him, Tom gripped him by his arm and as soon as Tom's fist closed around Ericson's wrist there was nowhere for Ericson to go. Tom pulled back his arm to hit Ericson a blow with all his strength that would surely kill him. Seeing this Lee quickly pulled up the tranquiliser gun and fired a dart into Ericson's neck. This stopped Tom from killing him, as Lee feared the act would steal a little bit of his brother's humanity.

Before Ericson passed out Lee whispered in his ear, "You are fast, but not fast enough…"

Tom stood up and turned to his brother in utter disbelief, grabbed hold of him and embraced him. Tom released him from his grasp and exclaimed worriedly, "How are you here? How did you find me?"

Lee spoke reassuringly, "It doesn't really matter right now, all you need to know is that I am and we are getting out of here…"

Tom looked down at Lee's feet and laughed, "Where are your shoes?"

Lee glanced behind him at the door lying busted into pieces and a large chunk of wall missing, then pointed to Tom's bare feet and replied, "Eh, where are yours?" The two men laughed then, Tom turned and grabbed his boots and hurriedly stuck his feet into them. Running down to the cell where he had made his entrance and grabbed his own boots and began to put them on.

Lee popped his head out through the door to see where his brother was. He saw Tom down at the security desk searching for something and called down to him, "Hurry up Tom, come this way…"

Tom glimpsed down the corridor at him confused, "That's just a cell…"

With a frustrated look on his face Lee asserted, "Look I'm the one that just broke in here, will you trust me to get you out and not argue, come on!"

Tom's eyes were still scanning the desk when he exclaimed, "I can't see it."

"See what?"

Tom continued to look and with a muffled roar he shouted out, "I can't see the release for the other cell, we can't leave without McKay. He's in the cell next to mine…"

Lee instantly gazed over at the middle cell and saw a face pressed up against the glass watching everything unfold. Lee turned to his brother and with an exhaustive tone instructed Tom, "Just kick the damn thing."

Tom replied, "I might alert the guards. It's too risky to do it again." With that, Tom flicked a switch on the desk. "It doesn't matter, found it…" and the door to McKay's cell opened. From the shadows emerged the figure of the man Lee was trying to identify through the darkness.

This was the first time that the two had met or even seen each other, but each knew about the other from stories Tom had told. Tom introduced the two. "McKay this is my brother Lee…" then turning to Lee he said, "Lee this is my brother in arms McKay…" Lee offered McKay a subtle nod of his head in acknowledgment of his presence.

McKay scanned around the room declaring, "Man, you can certainly make an entrance…" Lee didn't like the vibe that McKay was projecting; sensing a certain amount of passive aggression in the way that McKay carried himself. The way he looked at Lee did not sit easy with him, it was as if McKay was aggressively scrutinising him, analysing him, but trusting his brother and wanting to make hast with their escape Lee instructed the men.

"Follow me, we don't have much time…" and he turned in the direction of the cell that he had used to enter the compound.

Lee made Tom climb up the rope that he had left secured to the top of the ventilation shaft and told him to wait at the top for him. McKay followed close behind; lastly Lee entered the shaft and carefully closed the vent behind him, being careful to screw back in the cover he had previously removed.

McKay, with a muted voice, called down the shaft to him, "They are going to notice we are not there, especially as you two decided to destroy the cells."

Lee looked back over his shoulder. "Well at least they won't know how we got in or out." Lee slowly pulled himself up the rope and into the vent.

The three men made their way back along the shaft with Lee guiding them to where he had entered. Lee climbed out of the shaft and into the night air followed by Tom and then by McKay. The three men were now hidden behind the unit that Lee had hidden behind before he made his entrance.

He instructed Tom to watch him make his escape out between the fences that he had entered through earlier and to await his signal to follow. Lee, showing Tom a dull red flashlight, told him, "This light is the signal; the fog will affect the light so it will appear even duller and mask it. When you see it, trace my steps. Be careful to stay out of sight. The light shouldn't appear too obvious to the patrol guards…" Once again Lee made his way to under the guard tower, timing his exit by the position of the light and the distance of the guards to him.

Passing under the first fence and crawling his way across the gap to the second, he slowly ejected himself under the second fence and into relative safety, putting a little distance between himself and the fence before giving the signal. Making himself small to the ground and using the fog once again to hide his position, he turned, faced the compound and gave the signal. From where the two men were positioned the signal shone like a red hew against the fog.

Waiting anxiously for his brother to make his escape, Lee knew that given his background he would make it out okay, but was unsure of McKay's ability to go undetected. Sitting on the damp ground, he tentatively waited to see who emerged out of the fog. While waiting, Lee heard a loud hissing noise come from his pocket and quickly scrambled to grab the radio he had taken from

Ericson. Struggling to get the radio from his pocket and turn it down, he heard command looking for Ericson to check in again.

"God damn it, Ericson you were supposed to check in ten minutes ago, over." followed by a brief silence. "Ericson respond, over."

Lee debated in his head whether he would answer in the place of Ericson. Lee struggled as to what to do, weighed up his options quickly in his head, recognising he had to cover up what happened to make sure his brother and McKay had time to escape. Placing his finger over the radio button, as he went to push down on the button a voice came through the radio before he had delivered his message.

"Right, Ericson. I am coming down, you better have a good excuse for that, over." Lee turned his eyes back to the fence where his brother was coming from and began frantically willing his brother to move with a heightened urgency.

Tom and McKay both converged where Lee was and

dropped to the ground beside him to keep cover. Lee turned to Tom.

"It's only a matter of time." No sooner than he had said those words a loud alarm sounded from behind them and all the spotlights illuminated the area. There was enough light to render the fog cover meaningless.

As the spotlights were scanning the area, the men found themselves pinned down by fast moving beams. Lee had run out of ideas. At a loss as to what to do next, he turned to his brother for guidance, "What do we do now?"

Tom grabbed the radio from Lee's hands, seeking the North Star to see where they were positioned in relation to the compound. Quickly deducing that they were to the north-east of the compound, he radioed, "Prisoners spotted on foot to the west of the compound." As soon as the words played across the radio the spotlights turned to the west of the compound.

Tom turned to Lee and McKay and spoke hastily, "This will buy us a little time. When they realise we are not heading west they will turn to the east, and we won't be there either, come on we need to put a lot of distance between here and there." As Tom stood up on his feet he put the radio in his pocket. "Let's go while we still have fog and the cover of night to hide our tracks. Come morning we will be easily tracked in these conditions." With that the three men rose and disappeared into the night.

CHAPTER FIFTEEN

Leading them back up the ridge Lee had maneuvered around only hours before, they made their way back to the ledge that he had originally used as a vantage point over the compound. Lee started to gather all his equipment that he had left before making his descent down the hill to liberate his brother.

Lee and Tom quickly began to hide any evidence that there had been a camp set up on the site and made sure to cover up anything that would link Lee to the escape. They covered up all his tracks so even though the guards would certainly send out a search party they would be tricked into thinking there was only the two prisoners and no co- conspirators involved.

As the two men cleared the area McKay kept watch. Noting how proficient Lee was in covering his tracks, he quizzed him. "Have you ever been in the service?"

Before Lee had a chance to answer, the sound of a twig breaking off in the distance could be heard.

Even though it wasn't loud, it echoed through Lee and Tom, reminding them of the imminent danger that a snapping twig can bring; a memory of all those years ago when they confronted the bear in the woods filling their minds. Despite being faint and off in the distance the sound penetrated the three men and caused them to instantly look at each other.

"There is no way they could find us that quick…" and in a deafening silence the three men waited to see what was to emerge from the darkness.

The men stood with their backs to the ridge and faced into the wooded area. They scanned the tree line for any signs of movement. Something caught Lee's attention away from the tree line. Glancing on the ground at where his equipment was he saw that all the schematics were sitting beside his bag, which had been moved. He turned his attention to alert Tom and let out a whisper in his direction. "Tom…" Getting no acknowledgment that Tom had heard what he said he again tried with more urgency in his call, "Psst, Tom…"

Tom then broke his attention away from scanning the horizon where he was trying to figure out who or what was there, and turned to Lee with a questioning expression on his face. Lee pointed to the ground where his bag had been opened and stated, "They are already here…"

Tom glanced at McKay and saw his attention was firmly fixed on the tree line. He ran up to Lee, gripped him firmly, dragged him a few paces over to the base of a tall tree and without hesitation he whispered in his ear, "Remember the bear…" and he launched his younger brother vertically into the tree over his head. Managing to grab a branch and pull himself onto it, Lee found himself half way up the tree looking down on his brother.

Hearing a commotion from behind him McKay turned

around to see Lee wasn't there. He grilled Tom, "Where's your brother?"

Tom hastening himself replied, "Don't worry about him, and just get ready…" Tom knew that the noise that came from the woods was too subtle to be more than one man and he was anxious that the figure that would appear from the cover of darkness would be the sinister form of Project K. He looked to McKay. "We have to get him before he gets us. We won't get a second chance to do this…" he fervently acknowledged.

Tom's worst fears were becoming a reality, as a figure emerged out of the darkness and began to move with the same sinister stealth that he had seen before. The shadows he cast seemed to come from three different places at once. The two men waited in the clearing with baited breath to see who would show themselves from behind the shadows.

A dark figure began to form and manifest. It moved out towards the two men. Even the fog parted to allow the man through for fear of the effect he would have. As the fog parted it was replaced with an ominous downpour of rain. The moon shone through and illuminated from the back of the man's head. The rain bounced off his body as if it was trying to escape his touch.

It was then Tom could see the same dark clothed man with the dark mask that hid his humanity so well. He seemed to be of another world, a cold world; a dark place where there was no weakness and if there was it wouldn't last for too long. It was Project K.

The man stepped out from cover and marched right into the middle of the two men and stood very still. Stepping back Tom and McKay allowed themselves room to launch an attack against Project K if needed. Project K tilted his head from left to right and assessed what the men might do from their positions and still made no move to attack them. Tom and McKay looked at each other at the same time and gave a small nod and then progressed towards Project K. The two men were skilled fighters after years of action in that army.

They engaged Project K in combat; Project K never

seemed to move, choosing just to stand there as the two men launched one attack after the other. Each time they came close to landing a blow on Project K he didn't seem to move, yet the punches never landed. It was as if they were fighting something that wasn't there, trying to hit a shadow.

Eventually Tom managed to grip Project K and with all his strength wrapped his arms tightly around him. Finally, he managed to hit his target and landed a barrage of punches to the face and body of Project K. Losing his strength and going limp he fell to his knee. Feeling this, Tom loosened his grip, telling McKay, "Quick, grab some rope, we need to secure him…" As McKay turned to look for rope, Project K's muscles began to tense up again. Rising to his feet, before Tom was able to tighten his grip again, Project K threw his head back and struck Tom right on his nose with the back of his head.

Tom's eyes began to water up and clouded his vision. As a result, he released Project K from his hold and stumbled backwards to re-gather his composure. Project K now viewed a n incapacitated Tom as less of an immediate threat so he turned his attention to McKay.

McKay was in a hurried panic and searching for rope.

He was unaware that Project K had managed to break Tom's hold on him and incapacitate him, nor was he aware of the immediate attack about to be thrust upon him. With very silent and deliberate movements Project K ran and launched himself onto him, unleashing blow after blow to the face of McKay.

Holding McKay up, he kept him from falling from his grasp but McKay's body went limp and seemed to be just hanging from the hand of Project K.

Tom in a panicked daze had just about been able to recover from the eye-watering blow he had taken to the face Looking up and seeing McKay's limp body; he ran over and gripped Project K from behind. This time instead of squeezing him, he lifted him up off the ground, turned him upside down and with gritted determination drove Project K down into the ground headfirst. Hearing an almighty crunch as he dashed Project K's head off a rock that lay at his feet, his body fell limp for the last time.

Any sinister signs had been removed from his body by Tom along with any signs of life. Tom dropped his body, which fell to his feet in an exhausted lifeless pile.

He took a breath to compose himself, for he had effectively defeated the undefeated. Then Tom began to think about this feat and something didn't sit right with him. Looking to McKay he stated, "That was too easy, there's something going on…" He went to tend to McKay, not knowing if he was alive or dead. To Tom's bewilderment he found him to be unhurt and unharmed and very much conscious as opposed to the lifeless body he had seen only moments before.

Tom paused seeing this. McKay saw that Tom was processing what he was seeing, with a reluctant and hesitant expression upon his face he assured him, "It's okay Tom, I'm a healer…"

Never knowing what McKay's ability was, this made sense

to Tom after what he had just seen, so he leaned over and extended his hand to help his comrade up.

While doing did this he called his mind back to his childhood and when his mother got hurt she would heal relatively quickly, but the greater the injuries the longer it would take for them to heal. It may have only been a matter of minutes, but she would still heal. Given the extent of the beating that McKay had just taken, Tom got a little suspicious and considered his surroundings. Looking over McKay's body where it lay, he realised something was missing and with trepidation questioned, "Where is the blood, McKay?"

There was a pause as McKay looked up at him from the ground. Tom leant down, taking McKay by the hand and began to help him to his feet before challenging him. "Where is the blood, even healers bleed the same, they just heal faster…" As Tom raised McKay up from the ground, noise crackled from the radio he had taken from Lee earlier.

There was no voice on the other end of the radio waiting

for someone to check in; this time Tom just heard radio interference. Looking down to where the noise was coming from he realised that the radio placed on his hip was touching against McKay. Bringing his eyes to meet McKay's with sudden, wounded clarity. "It's you." Gasping, "They tracked you. That's how they found us so quickly…"

McKay's demeanour then turned as an evil glare came over his face. Before Tom had time to act upon what he saw, McKay had stuck his two fists into the gut of Tom and sent him hurtling back from where he stood. Tom fell to the ground and endured a cataclysmic pain he had never experienced before. It seared through his body like a dull blunt electrocution. Tom struggled to get to his feet on the wet ground; falling again and the ground seemed to move under him. He struggled to get up to one knee and looked over to where McKay was standing. He saw him lift the corpse of the man Tom had just killed, to remove the blood soaked mask from off his face and place it on his own. Tom in disbelief, gasping for air, spluttered, "It's you." Struggling to find another a breath to deliver the words, "You're Proj…"

Before Tom could finish his words McKay looked at him and sneered, "Yes, I am Project K. It shouldn't have been such a big leap for you to work out…" McKay reached into his pocket and removed a small GPS device; this is what caused the interference on Tom's radio. "They don't need to track me, I don't need backup, but I suppose they just want to protect their investment…" Breaking the device, he proclaimed, "Alone at last…"

Now with the mask both hiding and showing his true identity, McKay walked over to Tom, grabbed him and lifted him up off the ground. With everything he still had inside him, Tom drew back his fist and threw it harder than he had ever before at McKay and connected with his jaw. He waited for McKay to fall to the ground or at least loosen his grip, but he did not. For the punch that Tom had thrown was the punch of a child and had no effect on McKay other than to cause his anger to grow to boiling point.

McKay hit Tom and sent him falling towards the ground. "You clearly don't get it, your powers count for nothing with me, but I do like how yours feel. It must be immense to have this kind of power in you the whole time…"

Tom sneered up at him defiantly;

"I know exactly what your power is, you absorb powers from those you touch, that's how you can easily defeat anyone around…"

McKay laughed and jeered, "Well done, Tom. Finally, the penny has dropped. When I hit you, I hit you with *your* power. No matter what it is, I can turn it against you. All the power and none of the weaknesses…"

Tom, struggled to find his feet as pain coursed through him. "Then why pretend?"

McKay growled back with menacing intent. "Why pretend to help you or why pretend to have been locked up with you? Well that's very simple really, I worked with you for long enough to know that you would have taken precautions to protect yourself. I knew you would make a copy of the files I needed to get back and I also knew you would entrust them to someone. I wasn't sure who

you would trust with them, your father or your brother, but I

should have known that you would choose your brother. And to

be honest I didn't think he would have the balls to pull this off.

Speaking of which, I know you won't tell me where the files are, so

therein lies the million-dollar question: where is Lee?"

Tom wiped his brow, got to his feet, "Lee is long gone.

You will never be able to find him. I might be good, but he's

exceptional and no matter how powerful you are, he will not be

outdone. Trust me, I know, and if you don't find him, you won't

find the files…"

While this was all happening Lee was perched above

watching all this unfold on the ground below, unsure as to what to

do. Seeing the power McKay had in him, he knew that without an

ability he didn't stand a chance. After listening to Tom cover for

him, he knew it was not looking good for his brother. He watched

from above as Tom struggled to stay on his feet and McKay

stalked him like a predator pursues his prey.

McKay spoke through the rain below. "Well if he has the files then I don't need you…" He ran at Tom, throwing him into the base of the tree under which Lee was camouflaged.

When Tom struck the tree the earth seemed to move, causing it to reverberate upwards and it resonated up through the wood and into Lee's body. Looking down he saw there was still a sign of life in his brother who looked up at him from below and smiled through all the pain and blood.

McKay then began to walk towards Tom saying, "Wow, you are strong. I wonder how much you can take before you die. I'm betting not much. You know all those deaths are on you. You get that right?"

Unable to move, Tom tried to rest his body in hopes his strength would return. "I was getting my men out. I was on the bridge about to save them, and guess what happened…" McKay was now moving around Tom as he spat all his pent up hatred at him.

"The bridge blew up; I would have saved them all but I was on the bridge you blew up. Next thing I realise I am being carried away, while they die." Pausing and for the first time letting his human side be seen, he continued. "My men died, because of you. 14 lives all on you."

It was clear McKay didn't believe his own words and they were seeped in guilt, blaming Tom for his own failing. Guilt fuelled his anger once more and he turned his attention to Tom's broken body at the base of the tree. As McKay approached Tom, instinct took over Lee's body as it did all those years before and he launched himself from the tree and flew through the air towards McKay. As he fell he grabbed McKay by the neck and used his own momentum to throw him across the clearing and away from the injured body of his brother.

Lee now stood between Tom and McKay, staring McKay in the eyes and vowing with steely intent, "Try your best, but you will not put your hands on him again…"

He stood and waited for McKay to attack and as McKay advanced towards him, he walked out to meet him without any fear in his heart for his own safety. He was not fighting for himself, but rather for his brother and if needed he would willingly die to protect him. In this moment his motivations weren't for a greater good. His hunger wasn't to expose a cover up, and even his beloved Jennifer fell from his mind as he thought only about protecting his brother.

McKay swung to make contact with Lee but ducking under his punch he jumped into the air, throwing a punch of his own back. It connected with McKay's face in the exact same way that Tom had done moments before, but this time the result was different. Lee struck McKay who in turn fell to the ground clutching his jaw. McKay felt something he had never felt before, actual physical pain. He roared in anger and confusion, he could not grasp what had just happened or how it had happened!

Looking up in disbelief at Lee, he echoed the sentiments of Jennifer all that time ago when she first touched him, "What are you?"

Lee was offering no explanation, but from what he had heard while taking cover in the tree he knew that the reason

McKay was unable to use Lee's power against him was simply because he didn't have a power. He didn't have a weakness either, so in facing McKay his power counted for nothing. McKay found his feet and engaged him in a fight. Every time Lee landed a punch on McKay his face was a mixture of disbelief and pain. But for every blow that Lee landed McKay returned with one of his own. The two men fought a bloody fight, neither one of them wanting nor willing to give any ground to the other. They fought and fought for what seemed like an age, each equal to the other. Both men, bloodied and bruised, began to tire.

As the two men battled it out, Lee's mind was moving at a thousand miles an hour, trying to get to grips with this feeling of strength. To be the one with the power over this monster was an overwhelming feeling that he just hadn't expected. He'd spent his entire life feeling like a failure, like somehow he deserved to live an unfulfilling life because he didn't have the one thing that really defined you in this world; a power. After spending years with this belief firmly etched into his personality like a tattoo, now he was overcome with a feeling of pride as he came to accept that he was not powerless. He was the only one who stood a chance of defeating this monster.

Walking over and grabbing McKay, who was hunched over and sucking in air, Lee pulled him up straight and was about to deliver a knockout blow. McKay in desperation extended his hand out and grabbed the knife that Lee had sitting on his hip, pulling it out and slicing Lee deep in the face. He fell back clutching his face as blood began to pour out. This seemed like it would be the end of the fight as Lee could not see or think of a way out.

Lee looked to where his brother lay unconscious and felt alone and unprotected. Bleeding heavily from his face and knowing that McKay had his knife in his hands and would deliver his final strike, it was only a matter of time until his light was extinguished permanently.

Battered, bloody, bruised and exhausted Lee found his way to his knees. He seemed to just lie there as if to accept that there was no way back for him, resigned to the inevitable. McKay looked at Lee, certain he was defeated.

"It's a pity really. I'd love to know what you are…" He raised Lee's knife up over his shoulder, pointed it down at him while continuing to talk. "Well I suppose it doesn't really matter now any way. The better man won…"

Lee looked up at him through pain and anguish with rainwater diluting the blood that ran from him, and simply laughed at McKay. Laughing in his face like he had no regard for anything McKay could say or do.

Faced with Lee's repugnance, he faltered in his delivery of the fatal blow and roared, "Am I missing something?"

Lee replied while opening his jacket. "I'm pretty sure you did…" Lee's jacket opened and revealed he too was wearing a small GPS device.

McKay looked though rain soaked eyes and with a look of contempt on his face said, "Yeah… and?"

Lee smirked. "Look down…"

On McKay's chest was a small red dot from a hunting rifle. McKay took one look at this and tried to land a fatal knife blow to Lee. As he raised up the knife a shot rang out across the night and the bullet struck McKay on his chest close to his shoulder.

McKay, clutching his shoulder, turned and ran for the ridge edge. He seemed to throw himself off and disappear into the darkness below. Lee sprinted after him to the edge, gazing down, but there was no trace or sign of him in the misty night below.

CHAPTER SIXTEEN

Lee heard a noise from behind him and turned to be greeted with a familiar embrace. It was Philip, tracking his two boys once more like he did all those years ago. As Philip threw his hands around Lee, Lee fell under his own weight from a mixture of exhaustion and pain, caused by the battle he just fought. Lee whispered softly in his father's ear, "You took your time…"

Philip was concerned, asking his badly beaten son, "Are you okay to walk?"

Lee pulled himself together, composed himself and judging himself fit enough to walk said, "I think I'm okay dad, go help Tom…"

Philip let Lee go and turned his attention to Tom. He quickly ran over to him and threw the bag off his back to the ground beside where Tom was laying. Wiping his son's face, he shone a light into his eyes and then turned to look at Lee and with subduced reverence voiced his fears. "This isn't good…"

With white knuckles, Philip seized the bag again, tossed it over his shoulder and took a firm hold of Tom. He lifted him up from the ground and threw him onto his shoulder with ease, telling Lee, "If we are to save him we need to move fast. We need to get him to the cabin where he will be safe…"

The three men made their way back to where Philip had left his car. It was much closer than where Lee had left his so the two men ran all the way back. Philip carried Tom and Lee struggled to carry himself. After what seemed like a marathon distance run the two men made it back to the car. Philip secured Tom in the back; Lee climbed into the back with his brother and rested his head on his lap.

Philip jumped into the front and started the engine, before pulling out he turned to Lee handing him a phone.

"Call Jennifer and tell her to get my big medical bag and

bring it to the cabin. Tell her to hurry and to be wary, she might not be safe…"

Lee did as his father instructed, taking the phone and keyed in Jennifer's number, listening for it to ring.

The phone began to ring, but before it was able to ring a second time Lee heard the soft voice of his love on the other end. Lee told Jennifer what his father had said. "Jennifer, I need you to listen very carefully," he instructed. "I got Tom, but he's in a bad way. We are taking him up to the cabin; you remember how to get there?"

"Yeah, I know…"

"Well, I need you to go to Dad's house and get his big medical bag from his office, and Jennifer I need you to be mindful. We don't know who is watching…"

"I'll be careful, you be careful too and I love you and I'll see you shortly…"

Lee told Jennifer that he loved her too and hung up the phone.

His attention then turned to his brother, whose head was still resting on his lap. Lee looking down at Tom who just lay there completely still, with signs of life ebbing from his face.

Bloodied, bruised and unrecognisable to Lee, this gave him a numbing feeling of pain right down to his core, deeper than he had ever endured anything in his life. It was strange for him, knowing his own body was full of pain and numbness, watching his brother laying there fighting to live, he felt useless, u n a b l e to help him. Given half the chance he would have willingly taken his place.

Lee sought some comfort that the expressionless man that laid there was in fact his brother, as the reality of what he was looking at was completely alien to him. How could the strongest man in the world to him be so close to death? Lee ran his hand through Tom's hair, feeling that familiar texture of his hair passing through his fingers. It brought the realisation of what was happening, that this was in fact his brother, his best friend, his hero and he was dying right in front of him.

Lee kissed his brother softly on the forehead and felt a chill in his body as no warmth emanated from it. Lee feared he was already gone.

Through an empty stare he tried to catch his father's eye in the mirror and tell him that his son had gone. He looked up, but was unable speak; no words would form on any breath leaving his mouth. Each time he drank down air to tell Philip what was happening and nothing would come out. So Lee once again ran his fingers though his brother's hair and whispered in his ear.

"Come back, please come back, I need you! You're my hero and my best friend and I just can't go on without you in the world…"

Gazing up to the heavens, with tears flooding from his eyes he saw the boy that had helped to bring him up and look after him in school; the young man that told him how to speak to girls; the man that laid down his own life to protect his brother and was now unable to hold his breath, imploring to the heavens above, "Please take me! I will willingly take his place if you let him stay…"

Suddenly Tom coughed as if choking on something and a large amount of blood exited both from his mouth and nose.

Lee roared to his father, "Hurry up dad, we don't have long…" Philip accelerated hard and drove with no caution or consideration to anyone or anything that was on the road. The one concern and one concern only was to the wellbeing of his son who was in the back of his car, struggling to live. Making it to the cabin and abandoning the car where it stopped; he could see that Jennifer was already there as her car was in the drive. Philip jumped out from the driver's seat and lifted Tom from the back of the car and headed for the house.

Going towards the house, Jennifer came out to meet them. She carried a look of intense concern on her face as Philip heaved Tom up the steps onto the porch where she stood. Philip looked at her and urged, "Help Lee inside…" Jennifer ran down to the car to look for Lee, peering into the car she saw Lee struggling to move with his injuries and exhaustion.

She threw his arm over her shoulder, helping him find his feet and aiding him up the stairs and into the cabin. They entered the cabin just as Philip threw everything off the table onto the floor to clear somewhere to place Tom. Philip laid Tom down and began to examine his son. Calling for Jennifer to help him; she did as best she could.

All Lee could do was sit and watch as his body would no longer respond to his will. Sitting, he watched his father and his partner fight to save Tom. After an hour Jennifer came to check on Lee.

"Lee, are you okay?"

Lee broke down and tears began to flow from his face and through the numbing pain and anguish he was suffering he turned to her and begged, "This can't be happening, there can't be a reality where I have to live without him. He is my best friend, my hero and my big brother. Without him I am not whole, I am empty and lost, he's the guiding star by which I live my life. I would willingly take his place if it only gave me a minute more with him, just to talk, just to chat about something… nothing… anything… I need to hear his voice. I need his advice. He is my best man and if he's not here, nothing will make sense anymore…"

Hanging his head to his hands and with tearful sorrow he sobbed. "I just… I just need my big brother…"

Jennifer listened to Lee's barely coherent desperation and saw the pain in his face and leaned in to kiss him softly. She placed the palm of her soft hand on his face to comfort him, and then brought his eyes to meet hers. She softly wiped away the tears from his face with a loving caress and began to cry herself. This man that she loved more than herself, more than anyone before him, was in so much pain she could see him cracking before her eyes. She knew that he had already lived with so much pain inside him and although she might not know the full story yet, from this intense evening unfolding around her, she knew it was serious and she had to give him everything that she had to give.

Philip came over and sat by Lee, breathless and seeming to battle with the words escaping his own mouth. From behind watery eyes, he forced himself to acknowledge the truth. "There is nothing I can do, Lee. I think we have lost him!"

Lee took a deep breath, trying to process what was being said. But he could not.

Jennifer once drew his attention back to her and earnestly asked, "What would you do to have him here?" Lee simply answered, "Anything!"

Again Jennifer kissed Lee, this time she whispered, "I might not be able to take your pain away, but maybe I can give you your brother back…" She stood up and walked towards the table where Tom was lying on his deathbed. Making her way around to the other side so she could look Lee in the eyes warmly, lovingly, fondly and she affirmed, "From the moment I met you, I knew you were different. I didn't know how, and I still don't, but one thing I know is I love you with every breath I have. Every beat of my heart beats for you. I loved you when I said hello and I still love you now at the end, when I say goodbye…"

Lee heard these words, stood straight up through any physical pain he endured; it was secondary to what he had heard. Trying to make a dash across the room to stop Jennifer, but he was too late. She placed her hand on Tom's head and light fused her palm to his forehead. The skin on her face began to age and weather as if she were an old woman, the only thing that stayed unchanged were her eyes, which she kept firmly locked onto Lee's. Her hands must have only been on Tom for a few seconds but these seconds seemed painfully long. Breaking her gaze away from Lee her eyes rolled back in her head and with that she collapsed on the floor.

The cabin around Lee froze for a moment and all he could see was the bodies of Tom and Jennifer lying in front of him. The pain in his chest overcame all the other injuries that his body was suffering from and for a second his worst nightmare played out before his eyes. To lose one was unthinkable. But to lose both of them would surely break him in two.

Lee ran over, grabbing her as she lay on the floor, pulling her up close to him. Lee was beside himself fearing he was losing her as well, but instead of looking to a past already experienced as he had when Tom lay on his lap, he looked to a future that he was going to be denied if Jennifer died. Seeing the kids they were going to have; he saw the day they would get married with Tom by his side as his best man. He saw them growing grey together and he saw this disappearing.

Philip also ran across the room. Taking Jennifer out of Lee's arms, he blew into her mouth, doing this a few times until Jennifer let out a gasp for air as if taking her first breath after drowning. Her youth came back with each breath taken. She struggled to catch her breath for a moment or two and then focused on Lee.

"It's too late, there's nothing I can do, I can't bring him back…" It was right then that Lee also knew why Jennifer found him so special and different to touch. It was then Lee got a better understanding of what Jennifer's strength and weaknesses were, he could see it was tied in with her life-force and how it flows through her, but this was not really his concern at that moment.

Lee and Philip stood up and walked to the table where Tom was. Philip began to work on his son again to try to save him. Tom was so strong that even for Philip giving CPR was like trying to give CPR to a wall. Philip wouldn't let his son go and kept fighting to save him. His arms got tired and he could hear Tom's already broken ribs crack under the pressure of Philip's robust hands on his chest.

Tom's eyes opened and he looked at his brother and father. Looking them both in the eye without talking, he told them to stop and let him go. And they did. Philip's hands fell down by his side and he just stood looking at his big strong son. Tom's eyes rolled back in his head, and giving out a soft breath, he was gone.

CHAPTER SEVENTEEN

Lee and Philip stared at each other in disbelief at what had just happened. Collapsing to the floor as his whole world fell apart in that moment, Lee couldn't believe what was unfolding. Sitting on the ground by the table where his brother lay, he tried to accept that he was there but he wasn't, refusing to believe that this could actually be reality.

Composing himself, he mustered his strength and got to his feet. Fixing his view on the ground first, he then brought his eyes up as far as the table, taking another breath and looking up again, this time to his brother's lifeless face.

Lee just stared at the body that his brother used to live in and the deep sinking numbness he had experienced earlier just multiplied. Lee couldn't cope with this. Once more he walked over to where his brother lay and ran his fingers through his hair as if for reassurance that the man in front of him was actually his brother. Lee knew it was him, but found it hard to reconcile that he was there, but he was not. Staring at his brother, looking for signs of life that would not come, he felt someone's hand caress his and take hold of it. He didn't turn to see who was there, as he knew already it was the soft touch of Jennifer.

Lee simply stared at his brother and choked, "I'm not ready for this…" Each breath Lee now took with tremendous difficulty. Gasping for air again he spoke softly, "I am not ready to say goodbye…" Pausing, he wiped a tear from his face and whimpering said, "I am not ready to say goodbye and he's already gone."

Jennifer squeezed his hand reassuringly and just listened to his words. She was determined to be a rock for him, for whatever he needed and right now she knew he just needed her to be there. He just needed her unwavering support as he tried to get through this tragedy.

"He's gone and I never told him I loved him, I know he knew I did, but I never told him…"

Philip had already taken his phone from his pocket and began to let people know what had happened. Ringing the hospital where he worked, he requested someone come to remove the body. Ringing close family members, he asked them to spread the word to people who would be concerned. After he made a few calls he turned to Lee with deep reluctance, saying, "I know this is tragic. I know we are both dying inside, but you have to get out of here. There will be people asking questions and with your body as injured as it is, you need to not be here…"

Jennifer took Lee by the hand and led him away; she took him outside where he could gather his thoughts. Sitting on a bench outside the cabin, she held his hand in both of hers, feeling the sorrow pass through him with each tremor of his hand. This was only the beginning and she knew it. She had been through this pain before and it only got worse and never got easier. You just had to learn to make room for the pain in your life. But she was going to do everything in her power to help this man. Gently she led him from the bench and to the car, knowing that he could barely see what was happening anymore, as he was completely lost in his grief.

She took Lee home, tended his wounds, and waited until he was ready to ask him what happened. There was no urgency because no matter what had unfolded that night, she knew the feelings between them would be unwavering. But she also knew that Lee would need to process it sooner rather than later and talking it through with her was the best way she could think of right now.

Lee calmly told her everything that transpired that night, about how he found the compound high up in the hill, found and rescued his brother and that McKay used Tom as bait to flush out whoever had the files Tom found.

Lee fell asleep in his own bed feeling a little safer and when he woke he felt a familiar numbness. His eyes felt heavy in his head and sore from uncontrollable bouts of crying that seemed to hit him every hour. Pain still resonated in his throat; another side effect from the cries of loss. A deep pain was drilling deep in his head as if a part of his brain had been removed, his body was no longer his own. He felt detached from himself physically as his body went into autopilot and got up out of the bed.

Slowly dressing himself, his body still ached, but that was secondary to what was happening in his head and his heart. Making his way downstairs, he forced himself to eat some toast despite not wanting too. Jennifer was by his side every second of the process and looked after everything for him. "Where is Tom?" Lee asked, with need in his eyes.

"He's already at your Dad's place…"

Jennifer and Lee got in the car and left in the direction of Philip's house. As they drove, Lee gazed out of the window, thinking it strange how people were going about their business as usual.

"Do they not comprehend that the world has just stopped?" he silently despaired.

But they just continued about their mundane daily tasks. This was so surreal to Lee who just wanted the world to stop, if only for a little while and acknowledge what just happened; that there was a big hole in the world and nothing would fill it.

Pulling the car in at the house where Lee and Tom grew up together, Lee peered out seeing in his mind the memory of two boys going off early in the morning to play golf. The younger carrying the clubs of the older, just so he was important to him. He saw the two boys going off to school together with the older passing on words of protective wisdom to the younger. A comforting sadness passed through Lee knowing he would carry those memories with him for the rest of his days, but would never have the chance to make new memories or grow old with his brother. He would never be able to share new experiences.

He passed through the gate and walked to the door. Jennifer was parking the car; Lee turned, waiting for her, not wanting to go inside without her comfort by his side. As he turned he saw another memory, that of a young man walking up to the house carrying with him his army gear in one hand and a pair of shiny boots in the other, wearing a familiar smile on his face. The memory of that time passed right through him.

Jennifer approached him and gently spoke, "Are you ready?"

Dipping his head, Lee said, "I will never be ready, but it's still going to happen…" so he turned and walked into the house. Walking by the sitting room he sensed his brother's presence there and was not ready to face the reality just yet. So he walked into the kitchen and was met by a mass of mournful faces, each with a look of sorrowful acknowledgment for Lee's heartache.

Lee eventually turned and walked into the sitting room where his brother lay in a coffin. He walked up to the edge, but did not believe the lifeless body to be that of Tom.

The person that lay in front of him was pale and cold. This couldn't have been Tom; Tom had bright rosy cheeks and a cheeky smile. So once again he slowly ran his fingers through his short greying hair and with the familiar feeling of what passed through his fingers Lee was unable to fathom that he was actually looking at his brother.

Lee couldn't help but notice that the shirt Tom was wearing in the coffin was tight around his neck and he also knew that this wouldn't have been comfortable for Tom.

Resisting the urge to open the button to make Tom comfortable, he resigned himself to the fact that Tom couldn't feel the tightness around his neck.

*

The next two days passed by in a haze for Lee; spending most of the time stood at the front door, he greeted each mourner who came past with his or her condolences. There were people there he was sure had never met Tom before, but were curious as to what happened.

Lee greeted each mourner in the same way.

"Hi, I'm Lee, Tom's brother…" and then would usher them into the sitting room where Tom was.

"Tom's remains are through here, and there is food in the kitchen…" he'd say pointing down the hall.

One person interrupted Lee's greeting as he delivered the same words for what felt like a thousand times before.

"Hi, I'm Lee, Tom's brother…"

The man spoke over him, "Hi Tom…"

To Lee's surprise and amusement, he found himself responding, "No, no. I'm Lee. Tom is the one in the coffin…" Everyone around Lee looked in shock, but Lee knew that Tom would also have found this amusing and just laughed to himself.

On the second night Lee tried to get some sleep. Running his hands through his own hair, he was comforted that it felt the same as Tom's. Returning to his apartment, he laid his head to rest for a while, eventually managing to find some sleep.

Awakening on the morning of the funeral, he was unable to shift the feeling that he was knowingly entering into the hardest day of his life so far. Getting up, and getting dressed, putting on a new jacket that Jennifer had got him the day before; he prepared to bury his brother.

He sat a solitary figure on his bed when Jennifer walked in.

"It's time…"

As she said these words she saw Lee sticking the piece of paper that he had been writing on in his pocket. He stood turning to her and nervously asked, "Do I look okay?"

Jennifer approached, gently adjusting the black tie that Lee had put on and reassured him. "You look good."

They made their way back up to the house to say their final farewells to Tom. Everyone left the house leaving only close family to say their good-byes. Lee walked over to his brother, again brushing his hair with his hand, in painful understanding that it would be the last time he would ever see or feel the brother who had lain down his life to protect him.

As Lee focused on his brother, his father was approaching him and handed him something, which was wrapped loosely in a red satin cloth. Lee looked at it puzzled and slowly unfolded the cloth to see what was inside. There were two sharp polished teeth, each was long and jagged. One was fastened to a leather lace in the

fashion of a necklace. Lee looked at his father.

"What is this?"

Philip explained how he tracked them when they were on

the trail and confronted by the bear all those years ago. Saying that

he had their back even when he wasn't there, he carried the teeth

with him every day from that to this and it was time to give them

to whom they belonged. So Philip reached into Lee's hand, lifted

the tooth that had the lace attached to it and tied it around Lee's

neck. "The other one is for your brother, you give it to him…"

Lee slipped the tooth into his brother's pocket across his

chest in front of his heart and kissed him one last time on the

forehead. He whispered in his ear, "I love you so much." Standing

up, he turned away, letting the undertakers seal his brother away

in a box that he would never leave.

The coffin was carried outside and a few volunteers

approached to carry it. Lee made sure that he was there for every step. The physical discomfort of the coffin pressing against his shoulder seemed a relief from the emotional turmoil that was in his heart. Lifting his brothers' coffin up on his shoulder he began the solemn walk to lay him to rest. The people who carried the coffin changed every few paces, but Lee would not let his place go.

Lee didn't know who was carrying the coffin with him, as he couldn't see anyone's face through his own grief, carrying the coffin so his brother was sitting on his left shoulder, as this was a familiar feeling to have Tom on this side of him. Lee knew that Tom's ears were right by him. As they walked Lee spoke softly into the coffin begging him to get up and telling him, "This is it, if you don't get up now there's no coming back." No one else could hear Lee's quiet despair as they took a long walk to the grave to say good-bye. He had never felt as alone or empty as he did right at that moment, knowing he was speaking to someone who would never speak back.

When they got there, Lee and Philip placed Tom over the hole, supported by a few planks on the grave they picked out. Lee stepped back and looked around, this was the first time he could actually see the funeral procession and how vast it was.

There were more people than Lee could count, but there were no faces. Lee couldn't see the face of anyone other than his father who was breaking down with grief every few moments. Lee could hear him talking.

"I was there for his first breath and I was there for his last. It's not fair; he should be burying me…"

Lee's face was sore from crying. He stood back and listened to the blessing that was being cast over Tom's coffin. Enduring, empty and alone, sensing no comfort in anything.

He looked for loving eyes, but could not find them. His throat was sore and needed to be comforted. Feeling that comfort would never come, he broke down. As he did a familiar hand slipped into his and squeezed tight. The comfort he sought was standing right behind him and he didn't realise it. With Jennifer holding onto him he managed to say his goodbyes and to be one of the men to lower his brother down into the ground to his final resting place.

Standing up in front of everyone that was there, reaching into his pocket he pulled out the piece of paper that Jennifer had seen him with before they left for the funeral. Lee took a moment or two and let the morning wind blow over him.

He gazed to the sky and felt a small radiation of heat from the sun, despite the fact that it was still cold and there was soft dew that lay all round. After he took his moment he unfolded the piece of paper, then first looking Jennifer in the eye, then Philip and once more back to Jennifer and turned his focus down to the page. He began to read his own words;

Today I say Goodbye

Today I say goodbye, to the man who was the apple of my eye

I take you here to your resting place and I hope you now find
eternal grace.

Willingly I walk the path that you have walked, guided by your light
I shall never be lost

I carry you along these final steps, to this place where you are laid
to rest.

Not ready to say goodbye, knowing deep down inside
the reason why.

You are my hero, my friend; you can do no
wrong, even if you try.

I pick myself up and I will move on, safe in the knowledge we left
no stone unturned.

I feel you in my heart and your guiding hand on my back, but
still

I must say goodbye.
I will carry you forever and love you even
longer but on this day, I must say

Goodbye

Lee tearfully struggled to force the words out of his

mouth. Talking to Tom and for all to hear, he made it through and

delivered the words he wanted to say to his big brother.

Maintaining a strong jaw despite the emotions bubbling through

him, he bid his final farewells to all the mourners who had come

to see Tom off.

Lee, Jennifer and Philip returned to the house and to their

new reality; a world where a good man was taken so early and for

no good reason.

CHAPTER EIGHTEEN

Over the coming weeks Lee healed physically from the injuries sustained during the fight, but he was left with a scar across his face from where McKay cut him. It would serve as a constant reminder of what he endured to survive, although physically he healed relatively quickly under the care of Jennifer and his father. But the reality was that no matter how much time passed, the acute pain of the loss of his brother would never leave him. It would remain etched into his skin and his bones, just like the scar on his face. And he wouldn't have it any other way.

Philip procured another wrecked shell of a car and spent most of his time between working on restoring it and tending to Lee when he needed. Philip seemed to have an incredible burst of energy over the following weeks, never stopping to take account of what happened, fully restoring the vehicle in a matter of weeks. Lee and

Jennifer knew that he was just trying to avoid the chaos he had inside. They were each suffering and dealing with it in their own way and just hoping that soon they would see the light at the other side.

Emotionally finding himself lost, the prospects of a world without Tom's guiding presence were too much for Lee to endure. Everywhere Lee looked he saw Tom's face, in every movement he made, in everything that was around him; it was both a comfort and a curse, willingly carrying this sadness with him. He wished his brother was still there, but remembered that he had no regrets in their relationship. Comforted that his brother was his best friend, there was nothing more he could have done to be closer to him in his lifetime.

But he also knew that he was taken away before his time and someone had to answer for what had transpired. He resented the fact that his brother was taken from him and trying to hide this made him very moody and easily agitated. This was the wrong way to be, but he just had to get through what he was feeling, because deep down even though he wished his brother was there and wished he could have taken his place, he knew that Tom would only have ever wanted him to live a long and happy life. Lee sat on the couch in the sitting room, unable to communicate through the relentless pain that surged through his veins. Jennifer came in and sat beside him. She didn't talk as she waited for Lee to speak first, to see if he was able to open up a little. But he did not move. He just sat in silence, numbed by pain. Jennifer could see he was not going to talk, not yet. She flicked on the TV and turned on a film she knew Lee always loved. Lee became visibly agitated and uncomfortable. By the time the opening credits finished, he was rubbing his eyes and hiding his face. Jennifer hesitantly asked, "Are you ok?"

Lee did something he had not done before, snapping at her, "How could I be ok? Tom is dead. Do you not get that? He's gone and I will never see him again. I will never hear his voice. I will never confide in him. And I will never watch our favourite film together again!" He gestured towards the TV.

Jennifer knew that the film triggered this and that it was not a personal slight against her. But still it stung as she was trying her best to be there for him and give him everything he needed. She bit her lip and looked at her hands, trying to work out what to do; how to help this man that she loved who was in so much pain. Looking up at him with wide eyes she caught a glimmer of the man behind the pain and found the strength inside to reason with herself that it would take time. She stood up and threw her arms around him, kissing his cheek.

"You will be ok. I promise you!"

Lee took as much comfort in the words as he could and with a cracking voice, "I am sorry, it's not easy!"

The only people who could link him to the breakout and Tom's death was Tom, who he just buried and McKay, who was dead.

Impatient with the recovery process and willing himself to heal faster he became frustrated and a restless energy built up inside of him. Lee needed an outlet to focus his attention on and build up the strength within him to face the task of exposing the atrocities that the United New World had been involved in and the subsequent cover-ups. Lee gathered the files that his brother uncovered from where he stashed them, under the floorboards in the spare room of his apartment, and began to work.

Studying the notes, he learned the entire truth of what had been happening and how the government had been both dictating to and controlling the international media. He learned that there was a specific chain of command within the government and the cover-ups went right to the highest office in the land.

Lee pieced all the information together and wrote his article, exposing the full extent of what happened with irrefutable evidence, including names of high ranking officials and specific events that were covered up and why. It explained that the media was fed mistruths about the state of things in the economy to ensure a stability mechanism.

He worked tirelessly on his article day and night, writing and rewriting sentences. Changing the structure, the opening line, and the headline. It had to be perfect and there was no room for mistakes. After two weeks of constant grind he finally had a finished article. It extensively exposed all the corruption and cover-ups that were contained in the files. Rarely taking time to relax he seemed to use the article as a method of cleansing; a way to connect with Tom. A way to help him put some reason to his death and to help bring a little justice to what had happened.

When finished, he informed his boss, Pete Laurie that the article was complete, informing him how long the article was and of the specifics of sneaking the article into the paper without raising any alarms. It was arranged that Lee would sneak into Pete's office on Friday; Pete would slip out early, before the paper went to print. That way he could insert the story and have it as the lead article for the weekend edition.

Lee did this with relative ease and went home to wait and see what would come of his article.

Going to sleep that night, he expectantly awaited the early edition of the paper to reach him by 7am. However, at 4am Lee heard a loud bang on the door and went to see what it was.

Opening the door and peering outside, his eyes searched the area for signs of life, there were none to be seen anywhere. Looking down he saw a copy of the post with a note attached to it. Lifting the paper, bemused that it was there over three hours before it was due, he slipped off the band that held the paper folded and kept the note from falling away. At first glance the note was just a page folded in half. He unfolded it, looking to see what it said.

It only had one word written on it.

"RUN!"

Startled by this, he turned his eyes to the paper gripped underneath the note. He quickly read the lead article headline and to his surprise it was not that article he had written, but rather it read, "Local man wanted for questioning over disappearing soldier and in relation to the death of brother." and under the headline there was a picture of Lee.

A gut wrenching feeling of panic set in Lee. Turning to go back into the house to wake Jennifer, he hesitated, thinking there was only a small window to get to safety. He considered that if he told Jennifer where he was, he would make her an accessory to any crime they were going to pin on him.

Lifting his keys, he drove off into the early morning. Driving straight to the cabin, it only took him a short time to get there. When there it was his intention to lay low and see how things would unfold over the coming days. He drove up the lane to the cabin, parking his car and walking to enter the house.

Turning his key in the door his entire body palpitated with tremendous force as the door was blown out from the inside.

Such was the force that it sent Lee flying back off the porch to land hard on the ground. Lee, in pain and shocked by the force with which he was hit, looked up at the house and saw a menacing and haunting figure appear from the darkness within.

Lee was gripped with fear, unsure of who or what was there and waited for the figure to manifest. It was not the first time he saw a menacing figure appear from darkness and as he stepped out into the dawn's dark haze, the shadows on his face fell away. Lee once again faced the man in the mask, the man who scarred his face and took his brother away from him.

McKay had survived the gunshot and subsequent fall. Stepping out he slowly approached Lee. He was still rattled from the blow he sustained and could only ask, "How did you survive? How did you find this place?"

"That is the least of your worries…"

As Lee heard these words, the realisation of what was about to happen hit him. McKay was there to kill Lee.

McKay spat, "You know there was no one to link you to any of this and you could have gotten away unknown? But no! You had to try and expose everything. You had to push your luck and write the article. Did you not think we would see it before anyone else could? Did you not think we would know where to look for you? I am glad I found you here, it saves me visiting your home and making a martyr of that lovely lady you live with. Would be a shame if anything were to happen to her, off course if anything did, people would think is was you that did it in an angry rage! I couldn't

protect my men because of your brother and now you won't be

able to protect her, in the same way you couldn't save him." He

delivered these words threateningly as Lee got to his feet.

Lee stood, paralysed with fear; he was face to face with the

man that ripped his brother from his world. He turned his face so

McKay couldn't see the scar he had left there. Lee knew that there

was no way he could defeat McKay again as the last time they met

only the intervention of Philip had helped Lee to survive. Panic set

in and fear pumped through his body, he began to shake.

And when he felt like giving up he felt the physical

presence of someone else. A hand was placed on his back from

behind and without looking he knew who it was. A soft and

familiar voice whispered in his ear "You will be alright!"

Fear turned into a burning rage over what had been taken

from him and his eyes glazed over with a look of steely intent. The

hand that was placed softly on his back then tightened and gripped

the back of his top and strongly flung Lee towards McKay.

Without hesitation Lee bore down on McKay and launched himself through the air at him.

Immediately McKay was knocked to the ground and Lee began to hit him with his entire might. Sitting on top of McKay, he pulled the mask off his face and snarled, "No need for formalities."

Lee proceeded to unleash all the pain that was built up in him since losing his brother. Every time he hit him he had the fury of hell in his fists. He reigned down his punches on McKay; punching so hard he could not tell if the horrific noise of bone on bone was his hands breaking or McKay's face shattering under the pressure of his might. Lee did not relent and did not tire until McKay's face became almost unrecognisable.

When McKay was totally incapacitated, he put his hands around his neck and began to squeeze the life out of him. McKay was kicking his feet in an effort to shake Lee off, but his grip around the throat of the man who killed his brother only got tighter. Lee began to feel life slip from McKay's body and watched his eyes roll back in his head.

Before the life had completely gone out of his body Lee began to think of his brother and the man that his brother would have wanted him to be. Tom would have wanted Lee to be forgiving and compassionate, so loosened his grip from McKay's neck and stood up away from him. Turning and looking at the cabin that had been his sanctuary, he now knew that is was no longer safe.

He looked pitifully down at McKay on the ground, gasping for air and trying to get life back into his body. With aggressive intent asserting through deep breath and a grimace on his face, he spoke.

"I can defeat you, no matter what you do. You see how easy it is for me, you are nothing, you are just a bully and I will haunt you for the rest of your days.

Stay away from my family, stay away from me and I won't kill you. Go near them and you will not live to talk about it. I knew the minute I saw you, you were evil and I should have trusted my instinct. Tom would still be here if I did…"

Breathing heavily, Lee turned to see whose familiar hand had caressed his back and then launched him into battle. Turning, he found no one there. He was alone.

Running into the house Lee wrote a quick note to Jennifer and his father. He grabbed all his bags of gear and threw them into the car that his father had recently finished reconditioning. He looked around to see where McKay was, but he had already disappeared from sight and with that Lee sped off into the morning.

Jennifer awoke in the morning to find the place in the bed beside her where Lee would lie to not only be empty, but to be cold. She got up out of bed with a banging on the door. She went to see who was there waiting for her. It was the police looking for Lee.

Jennifer told them she didn't know where he was or what was going on. The policeman let Jennifer read the newspaper, which was tucked under his arm. As Jennifer read down through the lies that were written about Lee she feared for his safety. The police stayed for a while and questioned Jennifer.

Satisfied that she didn't know where Lee was they took their leave.

Within seconds of the door closing behind the police, there came another knock. Jennifer went to the door, cursing to herself as she expected it to be the police again.

"I told you, I don't know anything…"

As the door opened she saw Philip standing there with a tentative look on his face. Jennifer implored, "What's going on Philip?"

Philip gave no reply. Simply handed her the note that he retrieved from the cabin where he went expectantly to find Lee. All he found was his car, the letter and signs of a struggle. The letter read:

Dad & Jenny

I don't have long. I am safe. Don't worry about me. I have to go to keep you safe from what is happening. I will clear my name and blow open everything that has been going on. I have plenty of money and I am taking your car Dad, they will be looking for mine. I will be in touch, but right now I have to get away to keep you safe.

Look after each other; you are all that I have.

Love always,

Lee

As Jennifer read this, tears fell from her face for the man she loved. She was looking to Philip, who consoled her as best he could.

She spoke with an overwhelming sadness in her voice. "We don't all get the happy ending we deserve."

Philip looked back with saddened eyes and a slight curve of a smile and said, "This is true, but this isn't the end… Is it?

9 781788 080699